Copyright © 2024 by Mikaelynn Rose

All rights reserved.

The characters and events portrayed in this book are fictitious. Any similarity to real persons, living or dead, is coincidental and not intended by the author.

No portion of this book may be reproduced, stored in a retrieval system, or transmitted in any form or by any means, electronic, mechanical, photocopying, recording, or otherwise, without written permission from the author, except as permitted by U.S. copyright law.

This title is for adults only. It contains explicit sexual acts, adult scenes, and topics that some might find offensive. Please read the content warnings and keep out of reach of minors.

We've made it again! Book two was all my own imagination and it's been incredible to see what I can do. This book will have a significant amount more spice than book one, but it does make sense. There's still a lot of plot to this book, I promise.

Thank you to everyone who has been supportive through this entire journey and has helped in any way possible. I appreciate you more than you could ever understand.

Contents

Content Warnings

- Growing harem throughout the series

- Sexual content

- Mentions of kidnapping

- Mentions of sexual assault

- Voyeurism

- Jealousy

- Light BDSM

- Racism

Pronunciation Guide

Characters

- Aeros – Air-ohs

- Ahmeira – Ah-meer-uh

- Amara – Ah-mar-uh

- Amaroc – Am-uh-rock

- Ambrose - Am-brr-ohz

- Anevae – Ana-vay

- Azur – Ah-zoor

- Casimir – Cah-suh-meer

- Cassiel – Cassie-el

- Cordilaen – Core-duh-lane

- Eirian – Eye-ree-an

- Eiri – Eye-ree

* Emrhys – Em-Reese

* Eryx – Air-ix

* Maarya – Maur-yuh

* Maeyve – May-v

* Roarc – Row-arc

* Ruelle – Rue-el

* Viserion – Vi-sair-ee-on

Places

* Baeruil – Bay-roo-ill

* Caellaias – Kay-lay-us

* Ceraias – Sir-A-us

* Diathem – Die-ah-TH-em

* Dirsethik – Dur-seh-thick

* Eirvanna – Air-Vanna

* Ellaenea – El-lay-knee-uh

* Feraetheam – Fir-ay-TH-ee-um

* Haelian – Hay-lee-an

* Kaeuil – Kay-U-ill

* Kanlyrae – Can-luh-ray

- Kolathus – Coal-ah-TH-us

- Lamatorre – La-muh-tore

- Maiviraea – My-vuh-ray-uh

- Rilias – Ri-lie-as

- Rilvara – Ril-var-uh

- Tyrkenea – Tear-keh-knee-uh

Other

- Gaellian – Gay-lee-an

- Keozea – Key-oh-zia

- Nyrthym – Near-thim

- Orletaylaer – Or-leh-tay-lair

- Sollamthus – Sol-am-thus

- Zyelvris – ZIE-el-vr-iss

The Unveiling of Caellaias

Book Two of The Kingdom of Caellaias Series

Mikaelynn Rose

The Kingdom of Caellaias

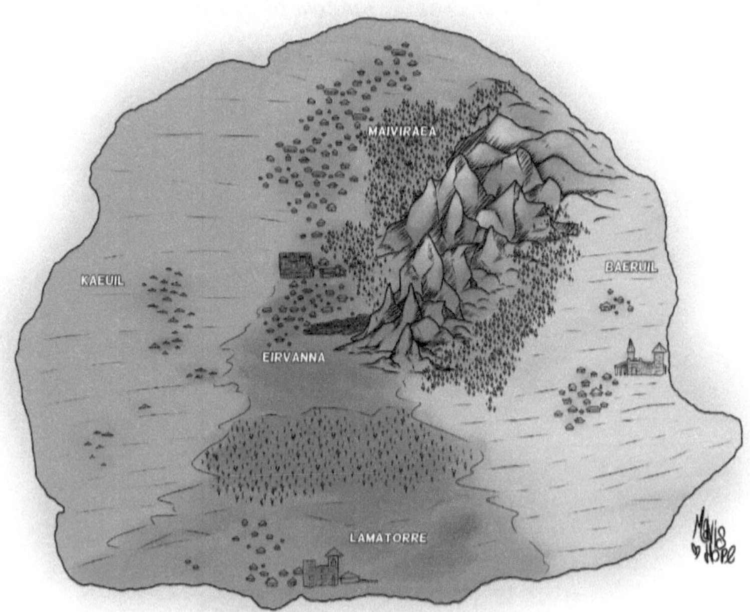

Chapter One

Anevae

E iri's voice echoed through the room as she greeted me, "It's nice to see you, Vay."

My jaw dropped as I processed the sight before me. When I entered Castle Rilvara's throne room, I expected to see my grandfather, King Casimir, with my sister, Eirian, as some sort of prisoner. Instead, she was sitting on a dark metal throne—one meant for a prince or princess—beside my grandfather. A bright smile was spread across her face, and her vibrant silver eyes glowed. She wore a purple silk ballgown that fit perfectly to her lean form, and her shiny silver hair was tied into an intricate braid. For the first time in years, she looked confident and comfortable.

I turned back to my grandfather, choosing to ignore my sister. "Now that you've gotten me here, what do you want? I'm anxious to get back home."

The king's yellow eyes widened as he lifted his hand to his chest. "That's no way to greet your grandfather, Anevae. I've been looking forward to meeting you. I've heard such wonderful things from your sister. She looks up to you, you know?"

Fury bubbled in me. "I don't care what you've heard about me or how excited you've been to meet me. I didn't even know you existed a week ago. What. Do. You. Want?"

"So feisty, just like your mother. My dear, I wanted you to see the world where you belong—your rightful home. You are royalty, and you do *not* belong on Earth with all of those disgusting humans," he said, voice dripping with venom.

"Eiri, come on. Let's go home. This is ridiculous. This isn't my home, nor will it ever be," I said to my sister.

My grandfather bellowed out in laughter. "Oh, sweet girl. Your sister isn't going anywhere. Right, Eirian?" he asked.

Eiri's smile deepened, revealing her sparkling white teeth. "Yes, Grandfather. This is where I belong—*this* is my home."

"Eiri, what are you talking about? We barely know anything about this place. I don't know what he's told you, but this is *not* our home."

My sister shook her head as she looked at our grandfather with adoration in her eyes. "We belong in Caellaias. We are nothing like the humans. I don't know what our parents were thinking when they ran off to the human realm. They were foolish to leave."

"Eirian, listen to yourself! All we know about this place is from the stories Momma told us all those years ago. I know our parents have kept a lot from us over the years, but she tried to warn us about this place in her own way."

The adoring look in her eye vanished as she laughed and returned her gaze to mine. "I'm not going back, no matter how much you try to convince me. This is where we belong."

I began stalking closer to the dais and pointed a finger at my grandfather. "What have you done to her? What have you told her?"

When I reached the steps of the dais, a guard appeared in front of me.

"Stand down. She is not to be harmed," Grandfather said.

As the guard backed up, I met my sister's gaze again. "I will not leave without you." Then, I turned my attention to my grandfather. "And I will find out what the fuck you're up to."

My grandfather laughed and said, "I have done nothing but tell your sister the truth and show her the place where she belongs." Then, he smiled, gave two loud, short claps, and said, "Maarya, please show Anevae to her suite and see the mutt out." His words dripped with malice as he addressed Maeyve. "Thank you for bringing my granddaughter to me, but you are no longer needed here."

I clenched and unclenched my fists. Taking slow, calculated steps up the stairs, the pitch of my voice rose higher and higher. "You will *NOT* refer to Maeyve as a mutt ever again. Do you understand? If you want me to stay for any length of time, you *WILL* respect the company that I keep. If you consider her a mutt, you may as well consider me as one, too; I am a half-breed, after all."

Before I could get any closer, the same guard from before stopped me at the top of the stairs, and I gave him a dirty look.

When I looked back at my grandfather, his eyes were wide. "My apologies—"

"She will stay with me—in my room—so I know she's safe," I demanded as I looked back at Maeyve. Her hands were clasped in front of her, and she was looking down at her feet, so her hair hid her face from my view, but I could feel her fear deep in my chest as if it were my own.

"As you wish, dear granddaughter. Maarya will show you to your room, and we will reconvene for dinner this evening in the dining hall. We have much to discuss. Once you reach your room, please let Maarya know what she can get you for lunch, and afterward, feel free to wander the castle for a while."

From the shadows to my left, a short, skinny woman with a pointed face and large purple wings sprouting from her back emerged. In a shrill voice, she curtsied and greeted me, "Your Highness, please follow me to your suite."

I dared one last look at my grandfather before grabbing Maeyve's hand. Squeezing it, I turned to follow Maarya to our room.

Fucking prick, I said to Maeyve through our telepathic mate bond as we exited the throne room. Keeping her eyes on the ground, she let out a huff.

From there, we walked in silence. I tried to keep track of all the turns Maarya took to get us to the grand staircase. The white walls lined with numerous intricate paintings of the kingdom should've made it easy, but I was too stuck in my thoughts to remember any of it. It was useless anyway; I had no intention of staying in the castle any longer than necessary.

When we reached the top of the staircase, there were three hallways: one straight ahead, one to the left, and another to the right. Maarya took a right turn and led us to the end of the hallway. Reaching the last door on the left, Maarya turned the knob and opened the door for Maeyve and me to enter.

The room was so stunning that as I stepped over the threshold, I came to an abrupt stop. The walls were painted a subtle baby blue with royal blue flowers and vines around the trim. The flooring was done in the red wood of the zyelvris trees outside. A seating area with two long, velvety couches and a matching armchair was positioned around a beautiful glass table in front of an enormous fireplace. Beyond that was a huge bookcase filled to the brim with books of all kinds. On the opposite wall from the door were two windows housing reading nooks framed by thin white window coverings. Between them was a massive four-poster bed that could easily fit ten people.

Near the window on the wall to the right was an immense marble vanity, unlike I'd ever seen before. Half of the wall was blocked off by paneled room dividers where there was some sort of shower, a sink, and a toilet. In the corner was a clawfoot tub that made the one in my cabin look tiny. Directly to my right was the biggest armoire I'd ever seen.

Maeyve released my hand as I stood there, glancing around in awe, and nudged me further into the room. When she got her first glimpse, her mouth dropped open, too.

Holy shit. She said through the bond.

Maarya cleared her throat. "Your Highness, what can I get you for lunch? You must be starving."

Blinking rapidly, I met Maarya's gaze. "Umm. Do you guys have chicken?"

"We do, Your Highness."

"Then I'll have that and some water for now."

"Of course, Your Highness. And Maeyve, what can I get for you?"

"I'll have the same thing. Thanks."

Maarya nodded at Maeyve, then turned to me and curtsied again. "Your food will be up as soon as possible, Your Highness. Please make yourself comfortable. There are gowns in the armoire that have been tailored to your size. His Majesty will expect you to dress accordingly when you meet him for dinner this evening. Please excuse me." Then she left and lightly closed the door behind her.

"Now, what do we do?" Maeyve asked.

I reached up to cup her cheek. "I can't leave without my sister. I'm sure you understand. While I would say you don't have to stay, you don't have much of a choice anymore. You're stuck with me forever." I said with a teasing tone. "I will get Eiri to go back home with us. I don't want to stay here any longer than I have to. And I don't want my parents to freak out. I scheduled a text to my mom to explain everything if we aren't back in the next week. If she gets that text, I'm afraid of what will happen."

Nodding, she closed her eyes and covered my hand with hers. We stood there for a moment before she lifted my palm to her lips and kissed it. Then, she turned toward the sitting area. She threw our bag onto the chair and plopped down onto one of the couches, letting out a long sigh.

My heart sank as I watched her for a moment. I knew she was uncomfortable being in Caellaias, and I wasn't quite sure how to make it better. I wandered to the armoire to give myself something to do. When I pulled it open, I gasped. There were dresses of all different colors, materials, and lengths. Some were meant for formal gatherings, while others were meant for casual wear. Reaching in, I retrieved one that was a beautiful crimson color—almost the exact color of my hair. Laying it out on the bed, I admired the intricate designs of it. It had short sleeves, a corset under the bust, and a ballgown skirt. The top was cut straight across so it didn't show too much cleavage, and small flowers were sewn into the fabric here and there. The corset was made of a silver mesh-like fabric. In the back, it was laced up with a silver ribbon. The laces stopped at the top of the skirt, where additional little flowers were sewn into the pleats and seams. It was beautiful.

A knock sounded on the door. Maeyve let out another sigh before she went to answer.

"Good day," a man said in a hushed voice as the door swung open.

The man at the door was short and elderly-looking. He was similar in appearance to Maarya, with his pointed face and large purple wings sprouting from his back. Unlike Maarya, the man's face was wrinkly, and his eyes had dark bags beneath them.

Before Maeyve could answer, he shuffled past her to place our food on the glass table. "Your Highness, it's a pleasure to make your acquaintance. Please enjoy your lunch and let us know if you are in need of anything else."

"Th-thank you. What's your name?"

He bowed deeply toward me. "My name is Azur, Your Highness. But please call me Az. I must be off. Enjoy." He rushed to the door, turned toward me, and bowed again before closing the door lightly behind him.

A look of shock passed over Maeyve's face as she glanced back at me. "That was...interesting. I'm not used to someone bowing after everything they say. That'll definitely take some getting used to. Should we get started with our lunch?"

Nodding, I left the dress on the bed, grabbed my food, and took a seat next to Maeyve on the couch.

Chapter Two

Emrhys

I stood beside Eirian as I watched Anevae leave with her pet. I wanted nothing more than to follow her—to be near her. She was meant to be mine by a cruel trick of the fates. When I became a guard, I lost all hope of finding my fated mate. But the moment I touched her outside the castle and felt the telltale tingling sensation run up my arm, I knew I was screwed. Not only was she the king's granddaughter—which already meant she was off-limits—but he'd asked me to abduct her from the human realm. I could never expect her to trust me after that.

I'd hoped it would be easy to dismiss the mutt, but with how protective Anevae was of her, it was obvious that something was going on between them. It didn't help that I could smell them all over each other. Jealousy began to stir as I considered all the implications, but I shoved it out.

Without a shadow of a doubt, I'd never get to have Anevae, and I would have to come to terms with that fact—no matter how difficult it was. But when she approached me, and I caught a glimpse of the mating mark still fairly fresh on her neck, the fight inside me began again—along with curiosity. I'd never heard of same-sex pairs being able to mate before, nor had I heard of someone having more than one fated mate.

I shook my head and cursed whatever god may have been listening. Being so close but not being able to be with my fated mate was a harsh punishment that would try my patience. I needed to get out of there.

Leaving my station, I approached the foot of the dais and addressed the king. "May I be of any further assistance, Your Majesty?"

"You are excused, Emrhys. Please be ready at seven p.m. sharp to escort my granddaughters to dinner."

"Yes, Your Majesty," I said as I bowed deeply.

Turning to exit the throne room, Eirian called after me, "Wait, Emrhys! Will you *please* escort me to the gardens? I still get lost every time I try to go out there on my own, but I just love it so much."

When I turned to face her, she looked at me through her eyelashes with a pleading gaze. Nodding, I bowed. "Of course, Your Highness. Let me know when you are ready."

A bright smile spread across her face as she skipped over to me and wrapped her arm around mine. "I'm ready!"

Eirian was a gorgeous girl with long, flowy, silver hair, almond-shaped eyes, a slender figure, and a beautiful smile, but she irritated me to no end. Wherever I went, so did she. She was worse than a lost puppy.

Looking down at her, I gave her a smile I knew didn't reach my eyes. "Let us go then."

We wandered through the castle much slower than I'd hoped. Eirian claimed with every turn we took that she'd never seen this part of the castle or another when, in fact, I knew she had because I'd taken her on the exact same route every time we went to the gardens. I wanted to give her the benefit of the doubt—she hadn't been at the castle as long as I had—but it wasn't easy when her sister was plaguing my thoughts. Along the way, I tried to be as patient as possible, listening to every comment she made and replying with as few words as I could muster so she thought I was paying attention to her.

When we finally reached the gardens, I led her to one of the benches near the massive fountain situated in the middle of the courtyard. As she sat, I bowed and said, "I apologize, Your Highness, but I must get going. There is an important meeting I must attend with the general."

Sighing, she gave me a sly smile and presented her hand to me. "If you must. Thank you for the escort. It was a pleasure, as always, Emrhys."

Taking her hand, I placed a kiss on her knuckles and bowed again. "Thank you, Your Highness. Per your grandfather's instructions, I will retrieve you from your suite at seven p.m.."

Turning to leave, I let out a heavy sigh. I'd lied about having to meet with the general; I just wanted to be anywhere she wasn't, so I headed back into the castle. I needed a moment and hoped to seclude myself in my bedroom.

As I approached the grand staircase, Anevae's crimson red hair came into view, and I couldn't help but stop to admire her. She'd changed into one of the ballgowns her grandfather had tailored specifically for her. The crimson fabric complimented her hair and skin in a way that took my breath away. The corset cinched in her waist and accentuated her hourglass figure. Her wet, wavy hair framed her heart-shaped face, which made her gorgeous blue eyes sparkle.

Ignoring how much I felt drawn to her, I hurried down the hall behind the stairs and headed for the barracks. I couldn't allow myself to get too close to her. As her magic awakened, things would become increasingly more difficult, but I'd keep my distance as much as I could.

The barracks were wooden structures that had been built centuries prior using the surrounding zyelvris trees. The deep red of the wood made the space look warm and inviting, but it was one of my least favorite places. I was always seen as an outcast, and when I began climbing the ranks, I'd been treated even worse by many of the other guards. After being promoted to working directly with the king, I was moved into the castle, just down the hall from the king himself. While it made sense to me, many guards took issue with it and saw it as special treatment. From then on, I got along with very few guards.

When I stepped inside the barracks, I glanced at the clock. I still had several hours before I was expected to retrieve the king's granddaughters for dinner, so I had to figure out what to do with myself in the meantime. I was still irritated Anevae had been coming down those damn stairs. I could've easily slipped past her, but I didn't want to tempt myself any more than I already had to.

Several guards sat at one of the long tables in the common room playing cards, acting as if I hadn't even stepped foot inside the room. But I had no interest in playing or even conversing with them unless I had to. Shuffling past them, I headed to the general's office. While I didn't intend to speak with him initially, I didn't want to risk running into Anevae or Eirian if I left the barracks.

The general's office was at the end of a hallway that branched off into training rooms, strategy rooms, and weapon storage. I had fond memories of those rooms as I climbed the ranks. Once I became the king's guard, I was invited to sit in on all strategy meetings and encouraged to learn every weapon that could be found on the grounds. I mastered them all one by one, which only made my fellow guards hate me more. But, to my surprise, the general and I grew closer. He was about the closest thing to a friend I'd ever had.

As I turned down the hallway, I found the door to his office was closed. It wasn't a rare occurrence, so I continued on. But when I was a few feet away, I understood why. The pants and moans from within told me he had company, and it wasn't wise to interrupt him. He was an attractive elemental fae, and most women swooned over him. Somehow, he was still unmarried, but I doubted that would have affected his ability to have his way with the majority of the women in the castle. He had little regard for a woman's ranking, marital status, or race; as long as they were nice to look at, he'd find a way to get them in bed with him.

"Fuck," I muttered quietly before returning to the common room. I had to come up with a new plan. Reluctantly, I took a seat on the unoccupied couch across the room from the other guards, hoping they would leave me alone. Apparently, that was too much to ask for.

"Well, look who the cat dragged in, boys." Viserion, a big, burly tiger shifter of six feet six inches tall with ginger hair and a full beard to match, said in a teasing voice.

"Haha, very funny. I'll only be here for a minute," I said as I glanced at him.

Not only was he looking at me, but everyone at the table with him had put down their cards to stare at me, too.

Great. Just what I wanted. More attention on me.

"We thought you were too good for us now. Not like we ever see you around here anymore. You're so busy working for *the king* that you can't even visit us," one of the other guards, Eryx, chided.

Rolling my eyes, I heaved out a sigh. "I've been busy. The king has had me running back and forth from the human realm and the castle, trying to get both of his granddaughters into Caellaias. Now that they're both here, one is pretty much obsessed with me and never leaves me alone, while the other can't stand me. Not that I need to explain myself to any of you."

Viserion huffed out a laugh. "You were all about the ladies not long ago—fuckin' every one of 'em in sight. So why aren't ya going after the one that's obsessed with ya? Cause she's the king's granddaughter? Never thought that woulda stopped ya before." Then, his eyes brightened, and a sinister grin spread across his face. "You got eyes for the one that can't stand ya, don't ya?"

"That's really none of your business, nor does it pertain to the situation. I will not jeopardize my job for a piece of ass. I'm sure you'd say the same if you were in my shoes."

All the guards at the table burst into laughter. When they calmed down, Viserion wiped the tears from his eyes and said, "Keep telling yourself that, Emmy."

Clenching my jaw, I shoved myself off the couch and hissed, "Do not call me that, *Vissy*. I am not your friend. If anything, I'm actually your *superior*. Lucky for you, I don't go around flaunting my title and all my achievements like some of you do. Grow the fuck up. I'm leaving."

As I took my first steps outside, a loud booming erupted from the other side of the castle. Was it an attack? Had one of the fae lost their temper? I wasn't sure, but I wasted no time rushing to find out.

Chapter Three

Maeyve

After lunch, Anevae took a quick bath and then pulled on the gown she'd laid on the bed. While I tied the corset, she stood in front of the mirror, staring at herself. I had a feeling she'd never dressed up in a gown so formal, but it suited her.

When the last knot was tied, I snaked my arms around her waist and kissed my mating mark on her neck. *You look absolutely stunning in this dress, love.*

A smile spread across her face, and she leaned into my embrace. *Thank you. I'm still never going to get used to you speaking directly into my mind. It catches me off guard every single time.*

I chuckled as we stood there staring at the mirror, admiring the visual of us together. My olive-toned skin, jet-black curly hair, and orange doe-eyes were a beautiful contrast to her pink-tinged pale skin, wavy crimson hair, and almond-shaped, blue eyes. I wanted to commit the image in the mirror to memory, just in case something were to happen to us. Then, I'd have a piece of her with me for the rest of my life.

Taking a deep breath, she patted my hand and whispered, "Let's go, sweetheart. I don't want to be stuck in this room any longer than I have to be. We need to figure out why my sister has stayed here and what my grandfather has told her."

Before letting her go, I kissed her neck again and whispered, "As you wish, my love. Let's see what trouble we can get into."

Hand in hand, we left the room and proceeded toward the stairs. As we drew closer, the scent of tarragon and leather filled my nostrils—the vampire, Emrhys. I would recognize that smell a mile away, even in human form. His proximity made me anxious.

The way Anevae stood up to him, despite being much smaller than he was, was impressive. She was my feisty girl, for sure. I did know one thing, though: regardless of what he thought, Anevae was mine. There was no way she was his mate when she already belonged to me.

His claim sparked so many questions. Could she possibly have more than one fated mate, or did I mate with her by pure accident? Or was he just saying it to get under her skin?

No matter the situation, I didn't trust him and was frightened I'd lose her somehow. Finding her true fated mate could end everything between us. I could lose the one good thing to happen to me, and I couldn't imagine a life without her.

Growing up, I always hoped I'd find love—that I'd find the one person who would be mine forever. As I got older, I lost that hope because of everything that had happened to me in the brothel I was raised in. Both of the women I admired growing up turned on me, openly offering me to a world full of bad people who took advantage of me. I was still a little girl growing up and figuring out where she fit into the world when Madam Tanith demanded that I be put to work. Of course, the one person I thought I could count on didn't stand up for me—my mother. Then, a few short years later, Madam Tanith stood by with a smile on her face the first time I was raped by a client. She watched as I flailed, trying to get the man off me and get to safety.

When he'd finished, she threw a towel at me and told me to get cleaned up for my next client. Then, she walked away and discussed the client's requests for his next visit. Back then, I thought love was something that would never find me.

Anevae changed that. The first time I saw her, I had hope. I couldn't explain it, but she woke the little girl deep inside who thought something was wrong with her and that she'd always be better off alone—that everyone was always out to hurt her.

When Anevae squeezed my hand, I realized I'd stopped walking. I'd gotten stuck in my head, and if I wasn't careful, I wouldn't be able to pull myself out. If I worried about every little thing, I would deprive myself of the way she made me feel. And I finally felt whole for the first time ever. I'd let myself miss out on the real reason I knew I deserved to be loved.

Blinking a few times, I gave Anevae a small smile. I didn't want her to worry about me. *Please be careful going down the stairs, and don't trip on your dress.* Letting go of her hand, I urged her forward while I tried to find Emrhys. When I didn't notice any movement upstairs, I began scanning the first floor. Taking a step toward the stairs, light footsteps echoed nearby, moving away from us.

Breathing a sigh of relief, I began my descent down the stairs behind Anevae. One of her hands was gliding down the golden railing while the other was holding up her dress to keep her from tripping, as I'd warned. Her hair swayed behind her as she admired the intricacies of the castle interior. The walls were decorated with rows of the kingdom's symbol—the orletaylaer—all in different sizes, the teal accented with black and gold outlines. Separating each row of flowers were alternating strips of black and white marble.

When she reached the bottom of the stairs, she let go of her dress and waited for me in the middle of the foyer. Coming up behind her, I placed my hand on her lower back, and she relaxed into my touch. I didn't have to use my calming abilities to ease her nerves; my presence alone did the job.

Looking left and then right, I asked her, *Which way should we go, love?*

She thought about it for a moment, then responded, *Well, when Maarya brought us from the throne room, I'm pretty sure we came from the right. How about we go to the left? We can see what's over there.*

Sounds good. I'll follow you.

We wandered down the hallway slowly, inspecting every room as we passed. I tried to memorize as many of them as possible so that I could get us around the castle without an escort. When we rounded a corner, we were assaulted by bright lights streaming in through an uncovered window. Once my eyes adjusted, I analyzed my surroundings. Beside the window was a single door with shiny, crackled glass illuminated by the sun's rays outside.

Stepping outside, I stared open-mouthed at the sea of colors spreading far and wide through a garden unlike any I'd ever seen. There were dozens of species of flowers, vines, and shrubs sprinkled about in the most vibrant hues imaginable. In the center of the garden stood a massive fountain made of sollamthus, surrounded by benches made of some kind of white stone, and on one of them sat Eirian, all by herself.

As soon as I spotted her, I glanced at Anevae, who was biting her lip and looking at her feet. *Would you like to talk to her?* I asked.

Nodding, she returned her attention to her sister. *I'm nervous. I'm still not sure why she would want to stay here. What could my grandfather have promised her?*

There wasn't an ounce of tension in Eirian's body as she stared into the distance, relaxed and unfazed by where she was. *Would you like me to stay here, or go with you?*

I think I need to speak with her alone.

I won't be far if you need me, love. Moving to caress her cheek, I pulled her attention back to me and gave her a small smile before kissing her gently. *If you need me, just tell me. OK? I love you.*

Chapter Four

Anevae

As I stared at my sister, Maeyve wandered to another part of the gardens so she would be close. I appreciated her willingness to give Eiri and me space to talk, but there was a comfort in knowing she wasn't far. My sister and I lived very different lives and had drastically different personalities, so I never knew how things would actually go between us. Of course, we were close, and I loved her dearly, but we hadn't always seen eye to eye on certain matters. I was afraid this would be one of them.

She seemed so comfortable in Caellaias, and that scared me. From the stories our mom told us growing up, the king was cruel—even to his daughters. What could he have told Eiri to make her want to stay in Caellaias? Did he promise her something? Whatever the case, I wanted to understand why she wasn't fighting him and what was happening.

After a few deep breaths, I approached my sister, cleared my throat, and asked, "May I sit with you?"

Startled, she glanced up. When she realized it was me, she smiled and patted the spot beside her. "Please, have a seat! I'm so glad you're here, Vay. You're going to love Caellaias; it's such a beautiful place. And everyone has been so wonderful since I arrived."

As I sat, I looked around the gardens before us, taking in the view. The plant life was breathtaking, expanding for over a mile in each direction and full of every color imaginable. Each section had a unique layout and dedication. The section closest to the castle was created specifically for my grandmother, Queen Ahmeira, who passed away when my mom was born. It was full of orletaylaers outlined by black and white flowers to create the image of an even bigger orletaylaer. According to my mom, it was my grandmother's favorite flower.

In the distance was a hedge maze I imagined would be easy to get lost in. The hedges were full of black and red leaves, unlike the green ones I'd seen in the human realm. They stood over fifteen feet tall, looming over anyone who entered. I wondered how ominous it got when the sun set beyond the horizon.

Eiri was staring at me when my gaze returned to her. Grabbing her hand, I whispered, "Talk to me, please. What's going on between you and our grandfather? Don't you remember the stories Momma told us about Caellaias when we were growing up? About how the king isn't as kind as he portrays himself to be. We should really go home and talk to Momma about this."

My sister rolled her eyes and scoffed. "Our grandfather has been amazing since I arrived. He's been welcoming and sweet, making sure things are to my liking. He watches over me, makes sure I'm comfortable and takes what I say into consideration. I can't remember the last time Poppa did that for me. No one has had anything bad to say about our grandfather."

"He wants you to warm up to him—to weasel his way in and make you think he's an amazing person. No one says anything bad about him because they're his servants. If they speak ill of him, they'll be punished. Momma would know best about how he treats others and what he's capable of. She lived with him until she ran off with

Poppa. You've only been here a few days. You can't formulate a proper opinion of someone in such a short amount of time."

Eiri ripped her hand from mine as her face flushed and contorted with anger. "Aren't you the pot calling the kettle black right now? How long have you known Maeyve? Less than a month? And you're already in love with her. I can see it with how you cling to and protect her. I'm sure there are things you don't know about her yet, so spare me the lecture. I've spent a lot of time with our grandfather."

"We are *not* talking about me right now. *You* have been here for less than a week. This man had you kidnapped, for goodness sake!" I yelled.

Eiri's brows relaxed, and she dropped her gaze to her lap, where her hands were clasped together. "H-he didn't have me taken, Vay."

Irritation turned to fury as I tried to make sense of what she'd said. "What the *fuck* is that supposed to mean? You came here of your own free will and *lied* to me?"

"I-It's really a long story that I won't be able to explain before you speak with our grandfather more in-depth."

"Speak, Eirian!" I shrieked, and my voice boomed.

"Oh, shit. Anevae, calm down. Please. I don't want you to hurt yourself—or me, for that matter," Eiri muttered with fear in her eyes as she tried to grasp my arm.

Jerking away from her, I shot to my feet. "You don't have the fucking *right* to tell me to calm down right now. I want to know what is going on here. What has our grandfather told you? Why lure me here under false pretenses?"

Anevae. Love. You need to calm down. I think your magic has begun to awaken, and you need to be careful. You don't know how to harness it yet, and I don't want you to hurt yourself or your sister.

Maeyve's voice caught me off guard, and I whipped my head around, looking for her. She stood fifty feet across the garden, staring at me with her mouth agape.

Confused, I turned my attention back to where Eiri sat, but she was gone. Anger enveloped me again as my gaze shot back to Maeyve.

What the fuck? She was just about to tell me what's going on. Now she's gone, and who knows if she'll be willing to talk to me about it again.

That might be for the best right now, love. Look around you.

Reluctantly, I did as she said. To my amazement, lightning was crackling all around me. My lips parted, and I sucked in a deep breath. *That cannot be me. There's no way. My powers are only just starting to emerge. They can't be this strong already.*

Emotions can intensify magic. You're also of royal descent. It's likely you'll be very powerful. Take a few deep breaths and try to calm down.

Closing my eyes, I focused on my breathing, willing myself to relax and think happier thoughts. As my heart rate lowered, I opened my eyes to find the lightning surrounding me, waning slowly.

When I met Maeyve's gaze again, she wasn't alone. Emrhys stood a few feet behind her, eyes wide and jaw practically on the ground. My face flushed, and I ran to my suite.

Chapter Five

Emrhys

Before Anevae and Eirian came to Caellaias, many of us speculated what kind of magic each sister would have, especially because they also had shifter blood running through their veins. It was possible they would take on the traits of only the fae or only the shifters. But like other half-breeds, it was likely they would inherit pieces of both.

Seeing Anevae aglow and crackling with energy in that garden answered one question—she inherited her grandfather's magic. But that one answer opened the door for many more unknowns about what other magic she possessed.

I stood there for a moment longer, watching the electricity fade from around her. When her bright blue irises, engulfed in a fading ring of yellow, met my gaze, her cheeks pinkened, and she fled.

Still awestruck, I hadn't noticed Maeyve coming at me until it was too late. She shoved me hard and bellowed, "What the fuck are you doing here? I had things under control, asshat! Now she's fucking embarrassed because of *you*. Haven't you done enough today?"

Because she caught me off-guard, I was flung several feet away, landing flat on my back. I glared at her. "For fuck's sake. I've been trying to avoid all three of you as much as possible. But when I heard a loud sound, I had to see what it was; I am a guard, after all, and I had to make sure we weren't under attack. What the fuck is your problem?"

A growl emanated from her throat as she stomped over to me. "I know what you told her after we got here. I saw the way you were just looking at her in the garden—the admiration and awe in your eyes. She's beautiful, and she's strong; I knew that from the moment I laid eyes on her. But she is *mine*. Stay away from her."

Relaxing into the ground, I let out a deep laugh. "Just because you mated with her doesn't mean she's yours; it means you've marked her. That mark can be removed in an instant if the king desires. She does not belong to you and never will, little fox. For whatever reason, she was destined to be mine. Fate is a fickle bitch because I know she never will be." I jumped to my feet and darted toward her until we shared the same air. This time, I caught *her* off guard—the advantage of my vampire speed. "You do not scare me. Not even a little bit. Now, fuck off. I'm already going to be seeing enough of you around here. And save your empty threats next time. If you attempt to harm me, this whole kingdom will come down on you, no matter who you're mated to."

We stood there for a few moments, both breathing heavily as we tried to settle our irritation. Then, she huffed and stormed off toward the castle. I breathed a sigh of relief as I assessed the damages Anevae inflicted on the gardens.

A few of the flower patches and the bricks underfoot were scorched from her inability to control the electricity, but that was it. The magic she wielded wasn't able to go far yet, but it was incredibly powerful nonetheless. I'd never seen anything like it—even when the king used his powers. However, I'd never seen him lose his temper, either. She was already more powerful than she realized. I hoped she'd be able to control her anger because any wounds she inflicted would take weeks to heal, even for those with accelerated healing. I made a mental note not to piss her off too severely while she learned to control her magic.

When I was done inspecting the damage, I went back into the castle. Knowing I still had some time before dinner, I wandered into one of the sitting rooms. Before taking a seat, I stopped at the side table where the king stored his liquor reserve. Even though he hated the human realm, he kept many of their liquors on hand, including my favorite bourbon. I retrieved a glass from the cabinet and filled it half full of the amber liquid—just enough to ease my nerves.

Being a vampire, I rarely consumed anything other than blood. Most food made me sick, so I avoided it. There were times, though, that I wondered what something tasted like, so I'd try it and immediately regret it. But I could stomach most liquids, and luckily for me, that included liquor.

After capping the bourbon and replacing the bottle, I sunk into a nearby chair and tossed back my drink. It burned the entire way down, but it was a pleasant distraction from the woman that continued to consume my mind. The very first time I'd seen her, I knew something was different with her, but I assumed it had to do with her lineage and the power flowing through her veins. I figured her power called for me to protect her as I did her grandfather.

When I touched her skin, I knew I was wrong.

Once I realized what was happening, everything made sense. It was why I'd started to feel calmer around her every time I visited her home in the human world and why I'd felt drawn to visit her more often than I was required to. It was also why I knew I could never harm her and why I knew I wanted her in our world—so I could be the one to protect her. I never wanted to let her leave my sight. It hurt me to treat her with such little disregard; she was powerful, and deep down, I knew she was destined for greatness. But none of that mattered.

Glass still in hand, I leaned onto my elbows with my head bowed. I couldn't stand to keep coming in contact with her. I was hopeful the king would adjust my station. He could easily move me away from her, and I could still protect him as I'd been doing for so long. I had to put distance between us. Otherwise, I'd never be able to keep my hands off her.

Just before seven o'clock, I got up and put my glass on one of the tables. The servants would take it when they did one of their cleaning sweeps through the castle. Straightening myself up, I hurried to my room so I could freshen up and retrieve the women who made my life a nightmare for the time being.

Chapter Six

Anevae

When I finally reached my room, I slammed the door behind me and collapsed onto the bed, tears rolling down my cheeks. Why did my powers have to choose that specific moment to show themselves? The minimal control I had on them made me look like a fucking idiot. And then Emrhys had to see me like that, too.

Fuck! As if his opinion of me could get any worse.

I lay there for several minutes, continuing to scold myself and cry, before footsteps echoed down the hallway. I didn't need to see her to know it was Maeyve.

She came barreling through the door, fumbling to close it before rushing toward me. *Are you okay? What happened out there? What did your sister say?*

Thinking about what happened only made me more upset. I wished I'd been more prepared for my magic to surface—to know how it would affect me—and what would happen when my emotions got the better of me.

It's okay, love. You didn't know what would happen. No one did *prepare you for it,* Maeyve reminded me, able to read me without actually hearing my thoughts, as she climbed onto the bed.

I tried to roll onto my side but couldn't. The corset top of my dress kept me straight as a board. Frustrated, I forced myself up and moved to the couch in front of the roaring fireplace.

Fidgeting with my hands to calm my nerves, I said, *When I was talking to Eiri outside, she openly admitted she's keeping something from me. She claims my grandfather is this stellar guy, and when I reminded her that she was abducted on his orders, she told me that she wasn't actually taken at all—she's here of her own free will. She lured me here, Maeyve. But why?*

Maeyve sat up and looked at me with sorrow in her eyes. *I'm sorry. I have faith that we'll figure things out, love.*

Sniffling, I wiped my eyes to clear the tears that lined my lids. *You sound so confident that we'll be able to. This is all new territory for both of us. The only thing I know in this realm is that my grandfather cannot be trusted. My parents left this place for a reason and did everything they thought was necessary to keep my sister and me safe. While I don't agree with the way they handled things, they didn't want us here. I have a sneaking suspicion the king is keeping who he really is at bay to make sure my sister and I don't believe my mom's stories. Knowing Eiri, she's doing whatever she can to please him, too. She wants his approval so badly. But I will not sit idly by; I will fight him tooth and nail. I don't believe a word that comes out of that man's mouth.*

Maeyve sighed. *You may be right about why he's not cruel to your sister thus far, but we need to be careful around him until we know what we're up against. Even with your mom's stories, we don't know exactly what he's capable of.*

I nodded and let out a long, frustrated breath. I wanted to know what my grandfather was up to, but I couldn't figure it out without talking to him and my sister. The idea of speaking to my sister so quickly after what had happened in the garden was the last thing on my mind. She'd betrayed me and broken any semblance of trust I'd had in her. I wanted to give her the benefit of the doubt and believe she wouldn't have lied to me unless she felt it was right or necessary, but her actions told me a completely different story. For the longest time, she was my best friend—the one I could tell anything to, the one that would stay up all night with me when I was going through a tough time, the one I could turn to when I thought I had no one else in my corner. She'd been there for me through everything—especially when I left Ambrose.

But she'd ruined everything we had. I no longer felt safe with her.

Even with the ache I felt at my sister's backstabbing, my mind kept circling back to my grandfather's plans with both of us in Caellaias. *One thing that I'm still really wondering is why he wants my sister and me both here. Could he just want his whole family 'home' with him? It's possible we're just bait to get my mom here.*

He has tried to bring her home for years, right? Maybe this was the best way he thought to do that.

I mean, I guess. But how did he find us? My parents have been able to keep us hidden from him until now. What changed? Why work so hard to get us all here now?

Maeyve climbed off the bed and came to sit with me on the couch, opening her arms toward me. *Come here, sweetheart. I know your brain is going a mile a minute, but there isn't much we can do right now. Let me hold you for a while.*

Flashing a small smile at her, I leaned into her embrace as my heart shattered into a million pieces. Even with all the bullshit I'd put her through over the days before we got to Caellaias, she'd come with me and helped me get to Castle Rilvara so I could save my sister. She'd faced her worst fears of returning to a world where she'd know nothing but heartache and pain.

For *me*.

From the moment I mated with her in that carriage, it became about the two of us. Our lives were now entwined, and I couldn't let myself forget that. She could be taken away at the drop of a hat, and I couldn't take that for granted.

I felt like the only person left for me to trust was Maeyve. Since we'd met—and even a little before, apparently—she'd kept me safe. She helped me uncover my family's secrets and process who I was.

And then there was Emrhys. Merely the thought of him made my heart race, which irritated me. I wasn't sure having more than one fated mate was possible. Even if I could, I didn't know what that would mean for me—for all of us. I couldn't control how I felt, especially if he *was* my fated mate, but I continued to remind myself that he had tried to abduct me from my home. I loathed the vampire, even though my body craved him. I hoped the king would keep him far, far away from me.

Being so caught up in my thoughts, I almost missed the knock on the door—Emrhys. It was time for dinner.

Thinking of the damned devil conjures him. Great. I'll keep that in mind, I guess.

Sighing, I pushed back from Maeyve and whispered my thanks before wandering over to the vanity so I could freshen up. I couldn't face my grandfather looking the way I did.

Knuckles wrapped at the door a little louder, and Maeyve growled. Stomping to the door, she ripped it open and said, "We'll be out in a moment." Then, she slammed it in Emrhys' face.

A smile crept onto my face as I brushed my hair. Seeing their interactions would be fun, no matter how things panned out between all of us.

Maeyve snuck up behind me and wrapped her arms around my waist. *You look beautiful as always. Let's not keep 'His Highness' waiting.* She rolled her eyes and kissed my cheek before brushing her lips against our mating mark. It seemed to become her custom—to remind me how much I truly meant to her.

Let's get this over with. I replied as I put my brush down and unraveled her arms from around my waist. I planted a quick kiss on her lips, and then we headed for the door.

Chapter Seven

Emrhys

I nearly ripped the door off the hinges when the mutt slammed it in my face. Part of me hoped the king would get rid of her somehow, but I knew how devastating that would be for Anevae.

Damn it. Why do I keep going back to trying to protect her?

Taking a deep breath, I rolled my head from side to side, cracking my neck loudly, which gave me a sense of relief. Since Anevae and Maeyve were clearly not ready, I crossed the hall to Eirian's door and knocked.

Having them so close to each other seemed like a bad idea to me. When things got hostile between the two—and I knew they would—it would be difficult to keep them apart. Anevae had already lost her temper with her sister once. Who was to say that it wouldn't happen again when she learned the whole truth?

Ultimately, it wasn't my problem, so I pushed the thought out of my mind.

When Eirian answered her door, I bowed. "Your Highness, I'm here to escort you to dinner per your grandfather's request."

"Th-thank you, Emrhys. If you'll give me just a moment, please. I need to finish getting ready. I lost track of time, but I will be right out."

"I'll be here waiting for you, but please keep in mind your grandfather appreciates punctuality, Your Highness."

"I understand," she said as she lightly closed the door.

While I waited, I approached the window at the end of the corridor. Evidence of the day coming to an end was seen in the vibrant sun hovering just above the bright red leaves of the trees, so close to setting and bringing about the darkness of night. The milky water of the pond outside reflected the orange and blue hues of the sky above that would soon turn to beautiful pinks and purples. As much as I enjoyed the sunlight and stunning colors that illuminated the sky in the daytime, being exposed to the sun for too long would blister any of my bare skin, and my vision would blur until I couldn't see. Depending on the severity, the injuries took days, sometimes weeks, to heal. Nonetheless, I enjoyed the views from the comfort of the castle whenever possible.

As I stood there admiring the gorgeous landscape, a door swung open behind me. Another followed only a few seconds later. Preparing to separate them if their reunion went south, I turned to face the sisters. Glancing between the two, I immediately recognized the betrayal and exhaustion in Anevae's sunken red eyes, followed by the sorrow and pain in Eirian's puffy red ones. Eirian deserved everything she felt. She'd conspired with her grandfather to get Anevae to Caellaias. Anevae came here fully ready to rescue someone who had lied to her and had no desire to be saved.

I hated that I was a puppet in their scheme. I knew Anevae viewed me as the bad guy, but I was just doing what I was told. Seeing her so hurt made me want to pull her into a tight embrace and take all of it away from her. She didn't deserve the pain that plagued her. It was unlikely to be the last of it, though.

I cleared my throat and said, "Okay! Let's get you to the dining hall. Your grandfather is waiting."

Anevae rolled her eyes and crossed her arms over her chest. Eirian stayed silent as she bowed her head to follow me. I honestly didn't give a fuck what Maeyve did. It would've been better if she didn't join us—the king's distaste for the mutt was sickening. I'd never seen anything wrong with half-breeds or those of mixed races, but the king was adamant that they were less than; his granddaughters being the very thing he hated hadn't changed his mind one bit.

The walk to the dining hall felt like an eternity, thanks to the palpable tension behind me. Unfortunately, it wouldn't be going away anytime soon; any chance he got, the king would attempt to talk Anevae into staying in Caellaias, which would never go well.

The thought of her staying excited me, but I tried to shake it off. With as much pain as I'd caused her—even indirectly—she'd never want me. But gods, I wanted her so badly.

Get over yourself, you idiot, I scolded myself.

When we finally reached the dining hall, I greeted the guards, and they opened the doors for us. I stepped inside the room and moved aside so the women could enter.

At the head of the long dining table sat King Casimir with a satisfied grin. "Darlings! I'm so grateful you made it to dinner!" he exclaimed as he stood to greet his granddaughters.

Eirian's eyes rose from the floor, and a smile spread across her face. She'd admired him from the moment they met. Rushing up to him, she leaped into his embrace, clinging tightly as if her life depended on it.

He's not gonna be able to save you from your sister forever, I thought to myself.

Anevae, on the other hand, had a look of pure rage directed at the king. Her full lips were pursed tightly, and redness spread across her cheeks. A yellow ring began to glow around her irises moments before electricity started buzzing around her.

But then Maeyve grabbed her hand, and the energy dissipated.

What the hell?

"Anevae, darling. Please come and have a seat here beside me. How wonderful that I shall have each of you sitting by my side for the first time. My heart is nearly full! The only piece of me that is missing is your mother…I truly hope she will come home to me one day."

Anevae rolled her eyes before proceeding to her seat, and Maeyve followed close behind. They'd learn quickly that no one refused the king's demands if they wanted to stay on his good side.

As Anevae approached, the king wound around the table to greet her. "You know, you both look so much like your mother—especially Eirian with her silver hair and eyes." He stopped momentarily to look back at Eirian, now seated in her designated spot. "I miss your mother dearly. It hasn't been the same without her. I've been so alone. Alas, now you are both here with me."

Again, Anevae rolled her eyes. She wasn't impressed with her grandfather, and that would infuriate him. He was always the center of attention and expected everyone to swoon over him. When he attempted to pull Anevae into an embrace, she slid into her chair instead. King Casimir laughed it off and returned to his seat without another word. I wondered how many times she'd be able to get away with that before he disciplined her.

When he returned to his seat, he looked at me. "Before we begin, I'd like you to join us for dinner this evening, Emrhys. Please take a seat beside Eirian. I have things to discuss with you all when we have finished the delectable feast the staff has prepared to celebrate my family's arrival."

Astonished, I stumbled over my words, "I-I can stand, Your Majesty."

"I insist, Emrhys. Now, have a seat before I change my mind. I am rather famished."

"Yes, Your Majesty. I'd be honored," I said as I hurried to my seat.

Before sinking into his chair, the king clapped his hands. "Let's eat!"

Wasting no time, several servants entered the room, hands filled with plates containing the family's first course. The food looked delicious, but I had no desire to be ill. I waited patiently for my own "dinner" to be delivered. I'd be given one goblet of blood while everyone else would be treated to a four-course meal. It didn't bother me; I was used to the treatment, and one glass was enough to keep me satiated.

When a servant approached with my goblet of blood, my fangs instinctively responded to the scent, elongating slightly and piercing my bottom lip. I hadn't fed since my return from the human realm a few days prior, so I was hungrier than I thought. As the servant placed my goblet on the table, I licked the blood welling on my lip to keep myself focused. The last thing I needed was to bite a servant while dining with the king. As the servant stepped back, I whispered my thanks.

The king attempted small conversations with both of his granddaughters, but Eirian was the only one who reciprocated. It seemed that Anevae had no desire to engage in conversation with him. Each time she ignored him, he'd purse his lips before returning to his dinner.

After the fourth and final course was finished, the king relaxed in his chair. "I hope the food was to your liking, girls. Shall we move into the sitting room so we can be a bit more comfortable for our discussion?"

Everyone nodded in agreement, even Macyve, which surprised me. I was inclined to think she wanted to get away from the king as fast as possible. The king rose from his chair first, and then everyone else followed. I was the last to rise so I could follow them all out. Another guard would be at the front to escort them to the sitting room.

I entered the sitting room last and did one more visual sweep to make sure everything was okay. It wasn't that I didn't trust the other guards; it was just in my nature. Not far from the fireplace, the king took a seat in his favorite black suede, wing-backed chair with a glass of liquor in hand. Anevae and Maeyve sat on a matching black couch on one side of him while Eirian sat alone on another across from them. An identical wing-backed chair sat empty directly across from the king. In the center of the seating arrangement was a sleek, oblong, glass-topped coffee table that was rarely used. The king's liquor cabinet, hidden in the corner of the room behind him, was never used by any besides him.

Satisfied with my findings, I headed to flank the king as I'd done every time I accompanied him to a meeting, but he stopped me. "This conversation involves you as well, Emrhys. Please have a seat," he said as he motioned toward the open chair.

I bowed, then did as he requested—with reluctance. His invitation to sit with them wasn't something I was used to, and I wasn't sure what this conversation could possibly have to do with me.

Once I was seated, the king leaned forward and looked between his granddaughters again. "Since you are both here, I have decided to increase security in the castle. I want you both to feel safe no matter where you go."

I wondered where he was going with this. I'd not been involved in any additional security meetings. When it came to the girls, I'd been involved in everything. I'd long ago become one of the king's most trusted guards. He'd assigned me to some of his most important tasks, including getting Anevae into Caellaias.

The doors behind me swung open again. Swiveling my head to see who it was, my brows slammed down. Aeros, one of the few dragon shifters left in Caellaias, stopped beside me. He was a burly man with broad shoulders who, like most shifters, stood several inches taller than my six-foot frame. His features—green-slitted eyes, sharp cheekbones, and scales along his hairline that shimmered like emeralds—were shocking to those who'd never seen a dragon shifter before. He caught the attention of many, and that gave him an over-inflated ego. His cockiness often turned to arrogance which was one of my biggest grievances about him.

"Thank you for joining us. You may have a seat with my granddaughter, Eirian." The king smiled brightly as he gestured toward the empty seat on the couch.

Aeros bowed and said, "Thank you for placing your trust in me, Your Majesty."

Once he had taken his seat, the attention shifted entirely back to the king. He crossed one leg over the other and folded his hands in his lap. "Emrhys and Aeros are two very trustworthy guards, and I have decided to promote them both to protect my two greatest assets...you girls."

My heart rate spiked. *Shit. Please don't do what I think you're going to do.*

"Aeros, you will become Eirian's personal guard," he said.

My heart sank to my stomach, and I held my breath as he turned back to me.

"And you, Emrhys, are assigned to Anevae."

Whelp. There goes my plan to put space between us.

Chapter Eight

Anevae

"**Y**ou have got to be fucking kidding me," I said with a scoff as I cradled my head in my hands.

"Anevae, watch your language. Spewing profanities does not suit a royal," my grandfather scolded.

I glared at him. "I honestly don't fucking care about being a royal. I don't plan on staying in Caellaias. I'm only here to take Eiri back home—to the human realm. I don't need protection. And if I did, I wouldn't want this fucking vampire to be the one to do it. I don't care how *amazing* he is or what he's capable of. He tried to kidnap me. On *your* orders, if I might add. I don't trust him!"

My grandfather rose from his chair, his hands balled into fists at his sides. His jaw was clenched so tight that the veins bulged in his neck. With each breath, his nostrils flared wide. If looks could kill, his luminescent yellow eyes would have bore a hole into me.

He stepped toward me, and I rose from my seat to face him. Most men didn't scare me anymore, so his intimidation tactics wouldn't work as he hoped. Even though he was taller than I was, he was a few inches shorter and nowhere near as muscular as the man who raised me. My dad had tried to use our size difference to scare me throughout my childhood and into my teens, but it never worked in his favor. Even Ambrose, who had spent years abusing me, was larger than my grandfather.

We stood there for a few moments, facing off silently, before Maeyve grabbed my hand and sent a calming jolt through my body. My magic had begun to stir without my knowledge. I sent my thanks to her through our bond because the last thing I needed was to attack my grandfather.

We'd known each other for less than twelve hours and were already on each other's nerves. Things were going to get really fun if we continued to butt heads like that. He gave me a smug look, seemingly satisfied that he had won that round.

He returned to his seat and picked up where he left off, "I will not be persuaded to have either Emrhys or Aeros drop their charge. They will protect you both with their lives; I cannot say many other guards would do so. I will not allow anything to happen to either of my granddaughters, especially since you've just come home to me. Because you did not grow up in this world, I have not been able to prepare you for the dangers that come with being a royal. From now on, you will not go anywhere outside of your room without your guard or another suitable escort."

Clenching my jaw, I chanced a look at Eiri. Her head was bowed, staring at her hands, but even through her silver hair, I could see that her cheeks had reddened.

"Anevae, since your magic seems to have awakened, I have arranged for you to start lessons tomorrow. Your sister has progressed quickly and is already much further into her training, so I will not be sending you together. I also do not want you to use your magic on one another for any reason. Aside from training your magic, you will also learn about the land that may one day be yours. I ought to throw in some etiquette lessons while we're at it. You are a royal, and you must learn to act as such. But I digress."

With that, I stormed out of the room. I couldn't bear to listen to my grandfather and his ridiculous rules any longer. I would not let him control my life; I'd rather have jumped off a cliff.

Behind me, my grandfather's voice boomed, "Anevae, get back here this instant. You were not excused, and I do not appreciate you leaving while I was speaking to you."

I was astonished at my grandfather's audacity to boss me around like I owed him something. I didn't care what his title was or who he was supposed to be to me; he hadn't earned my respect, nor was he doing a great job at trying to build it. Plus, I'd made it crystal clear that I had no plans to stay in Caellaias.

When I reached the stairs, a blur of movement rushed before me, stopping me in my tracks—Emrhys.

"For fuck's sake. Did you come to retrieve me for *His Majesty*? Look at you following directions like the good little *bitch* that you are. Hate to tell you, but I'm not going back in there. He's fucking delusional. I've already told him that I don't plan on staying—"

"Anevae, I know you're upset, but you haven't seen your grandfather when he's angry. *I've* never seen him when he's angry, and I've worked in the castle for a long time. Everyone who has witnessed his rage says it's not pretty, so please do yourself a favor and turn around. Go back to the sitting room before things get out of hand. You'll thank me later," Emrhys said.

Crossing my arms over my chest, I stared him down. His eyes were pleading, but I wanted nothing more than to defy my grandfather—to push his buttons. I wouldn't let him get away with the way he was acting.

But then, Emrhys whispered his plea again, "Please, Anevae."

Sighing, I mumbled, "Fine."

Then, I spun on the spot and retreated to the sitting room. As I entered, electricity danced across the tiny hairs on my arms; Grandfather was close to losing his temper. I wanted to laugh in his face, just to prove that he hadn't won anything. Instead, I held my head high and returned to my seat as if nothing had happened. Behind me, Emrhys followed suit.

"Thank you," my grandfather said to Emrhys. "Thankfully, that was the last piece of information I wanted to review with everyone. Emrhys and Aeros, your new positions begin in the morning. You are all excused."

Fucking seriously? He literally didn't have anything else to say? He's fucking ridiculous, and I've had enough of his bullshit. Let's get out of here, I said to Maeyve through our bond as I darted out of the room.

The door to my suite wasn't even completely shut before I began trying to rip off my dress. I needed to get out of it as soon as possible. Maeyve entered the room immediately behind me and rushed to help me unlace the corset. When it was finally off, I crawled into the bed and flopped onto my back. Then, I grabbed one of the fluffy pillows and covered my face so I could scream as loud as I wanted.

The bed dipped beside me, and Maeyve placed her hand on my belly—a comforting reassurance that she was there if I needed her. Despite the comfort provided by her presence, I continued to scream. Grandfather was attempting to take over my life when he had absolutely no right to do so. Between him and everything with Eiri, I was exhausted and overwhelmed.

When my throat was raw and my voice strained, I threw the pillow across the room and jumped off the bed, heading straight for the sink to splash some water on my face. The cold water was a welcome relief to my blazing skin, helping to cool and calm me. With a heavy sigh, I faced Maeyve, who was sitting on the bed watching me. Her plump pink lips were turned down at the corners, and her dark brows were furrowed.

I'm fine, love. I'm just irritated and don't know what to do to make it go away. There's this pent-up frustration and energy deep down that I can't shake. It's driving me crazy.

Hmmm. I may have a way to release some of that energy, she thought as her face morphed into the picture of seduction. A pulsing began in my clit that rerouted my attention away from all of my troubles. Then, an image flashed in my head of Maeyve lying on her back, naked and playing with her nipples.

Mmm. Naughty girl. I like your line of thinking, though, I said as I stalked back to the bed. When I reached the edge, I looked directly into her beautiful, fluorescent orange eyes and bit one of my piercings.

"Crawl to me," I whispered.

Chapter Nine

Maeyve

A s the words left her lips, my pulse sped up. I didn't like using my seduction abilities, but she needed a distraction, and I was happy to provide one for her. Plus, she became more dominant when she was angry or irritated. I'd never enjoyed being dominated by anyone, but she was the exception. I'd let her boss me around anytime if it brought her pleasure.

When I didn't move, her eyes, once filled with so much anger and anguish, darkened to an intensity that had me soaking wet in seconds. "Crawl. To. Me. Maeyve," she commanded, her voice a low, menacing growl.

Carefully, I rose onto my knees and met her gaze. The light above the sink illuminated her curvy frame, and I couldn't help but drink in her perfect body on display for me. Her creamy, pale skin beckoned to be caressed, so much so that it was difficult to keep myself from going straight to her.

"What if I don't?" I teased.

A Cheshire grin crept across her face, and my heart skipped a beat. As much as I enjoyed submissive Anevae, I *loved* domineering Anevae. She lived rent-free in my mind, and I never wanted her to come out.

"Then you will be punished accordingly. Take your pick, but do it quickly. Or I'll make the decision for you."

Without averting my eyes from hers, I lowered myself onto all fours and did as she demanded, crawling to her ever so slowly. When I was still a couple of feet away, I sucked my bottom lip between my teeth and allowed my gaze to drift down her body again. I couldn't wait to glide my fingertips over her soft skin and hear all the intoxicating sounds she made as I pleased her.

When I reached her, I rocked back onto my haunches and met her gaze again. "This seems a little unfair, doesn't it? You're almost fully undressed, save for those lacy panties I'd love to rip off of your body, and I'm still fully dressed."

She bit her lip piercing as she reached for me. "We can easily fix that. Come here."

"Mmm. Don't tease me," I whispered before closing the distance and capturing her lips with mine.

Leaning into her, I wrapped my arms around her neck, and she slid her hands around my waist, pulling me flush to her body. I couldn't wait to get my clothes off, to let every inch of our skin touch. I wasn't sure if it was because we were newly mated, but I couldn't bear being away from her; I wanted to have contact with her skin at all times.

Her lips moved against mine, and I weaved one of my hands into her hair, grabbed a handful, and gave it a light tug. When her lips parted, a small moan escaped, and I took the opportunity to bite her lip.

She inhaled sharply, then huffed out a laugh, and I released her hair. She rested her forehead against mine and slid her hands up my sides. When she reached my breasts, she palmed them and found my nipples through the thin material of my dress, pinching them lightly. A moan slipped past my lips, desire coursing through me at a nearly uncomfortable rate.

You're testing my patience, love. If you don't do something quick, I will gladly take control, I teased.

After a breathy laugh, she placed a gentle kiss on my lips and let go of my nipples. Then, she slowly trailed kisses across my jaw and nipped at my ear before continuing down my neck. Just above our mating mark, she bit me gently, which sent a wave of pleasure directly to my clit. I dug my nails into her bare shoulders, and she released the skin so she could lick a line back up to my ear.

"Be a good girl, and let me undress you," she whispered before taking a step back.

I sat on my haunches again, waiting impatiently for her instructions.

She gave me another once-over before approaching me again. Gesturing to my dress, she said, "For once, I'm glad you're in something so simple."

Confused, I looked down. The dress I wore didn't cinch in at the waist or hug me tightly; it was loose and flowy. As I opened my mouth to ask her why it mattered, she pulled the fabric over my head in one swift movement.

"Lay back on the bed," she demanded.

I was too turned on to fight her, so I did as she asked. As soon as my head hit the bed, she ripped my panties off. I let out a short laugh of surprise at her aggression.

When I tried to sit back up, her hand was on my chest, pushing me back down. "If you try to sit up again, I will tie you to this bed and leave you begging for me to touch you. Do you understand?"

My tongue darted out to wet my lips as I nodded.

"Use your words, Maeyve," Anevae demanded as she placed her hands on my ankles.

"Y-yes. I understand."

"Such a good girl. Where should I begin? I do have to say that my dinner was not quite as filling as I'd like it to have been. Maybe I can feast on that pretty pussy to fill me up the rest of the way." With every word that left her mouth, she inched further and further up my legs, sending a chill throughout my entire body. When she reached the middle of my thighs, she squeezed them and hummed. "Open up for me, pretty girl."

My body responded, bending my knees and spreading wide open for her. The bed between my spread legs dipped as she climbed up, and my body shook with anticipation.

"Mmm, it seems someone is very excited. Your clit is delightfully swollen, and your pussy is already dripping wet for me. I bet you can't wait for me to touch you," she said in a sultry voice before placing a kiss on my belly, just above my hip. "Tell me what you want. I want to hear you say it; I want you to beg for it."

Staring up at the ceiling, I gripped the bedding beneath me. I'd never begged for anything or anyone until she came along, but I'd do anything she asked without question.

"P-please," I whined.

"Please, what, Maeyve?" she whispered against my skin.

"Please touch me. Make me come. Do something. Please!" I begged.

Tsking, she climbed up my body until she could straddle me. Leaning down to kiss me, she ground her clit against my pubic bone. The lace of her panties rubbed against me, but it put the perfect amount of friction on her clit. Her lips parted on a moan as they reached mine, and our tongues tangled together in a messy kiss. Her movements became frenzied as she continued to grind her clit onto me, chasing her release until she was quickly falling over the ledge.

Breathing heavily, she broke our kiss and looked down at me. "Okay, I *did* something. Now, tell me what *you* want."

"Alright, smart ass. Did that feel good? Because if you're not careful, I will flip you over and take care of myself the same way. Then, when *you're* horny and dying for me to make you come, I'm going to leave you begging on the bed until you tell me exactly what you want."

Scrunching her nose, she said, "So feisty. I love it. Tell me what you want, or I'm climbing off this bed right now."

"I just want one thing...make me come. At this point, I don't even care how you do it."

Leaning down, she kissed me deeply, then said, "You're being a good girl and a brat all at the same time. I'm not sure I like it. But, you did tell me what you want."

I rolled my eyes, and she trailed kisses down my body again, stopping briefly at my breasts to suck each nipple into her mouth. Panting, I arched my back, giving her easier access to every inch of my body. When she reached my bikini line, she slid her hands under my hips and perfectly positioned her face between my thighs. The anticipation was killing me, and I wiggled impatiently.

"Patience, sweetheart. It'll all be worth it in just a moment."

Those were the last words I heard before her mouth descended onto my pussy, and I let out the loudest scream of pleasure that had ever escaped my mouth.

Chapter Ten

Emrhys

As I was getting ready for bed, a scream sounded from the east wing—one of the women was in trouble.

Cursing under my breath, I darted out the door and followed the sound. Being a vampire, I could run extremely fast and had exceptional hearing, so it took me mere seconds to realize the sound was coming from Anevae's room. Throwing the door open, I stopped dead in my tracks as I took in the scene before me.

Maeyve was lying on her back in the center of the bed, black and orange hair splayed out around her head like a halo, with her back arched and perky breasts on full display. Anevae was between her legs, devouring her cunt. She was almost naked, save for the thin piece of fabric and lace of her panties that barely covered her pussy.

Oh, fuck. What did I just walk into?

I'd never seen two women together, and fuck, was it hot. My mouth dropped open, and my cock instantly grew hard, thinking of everything I wanted to do with Anevae…and Maeyve. While she irritated me, I had to admit that she was beautiful in her own way.

When I didn't move, Anevae lifted her head to look back at me. Flashing me a toothy grin, she licked Maeyve's arousal from her lips and said, "Take a picture; it'll last longer. Or, maybe you could join us—fuck me from behind while I make Maeyve scream. I know you want to."

Shock rippled through me at her words. By the gods, I wanted that more than she knew, but I knew I couldn't, so I shook my head.

Shrugging her shoulders, she said, "Your loss." Then, she winked at me and returned to her feast.

Maeyve's moans grew louder as Anevae continued, but I couldn't make myself move; I was mesmerized. My cock throbbed as I watched the way Anevae was lying with her juicy ass up in the air. Her panties were completely soaked, and I had to stop myself from ripping them off her. If I did, I worried I'd do something I would regret—like marking her. Or fucking her so hard she wouldn't be able to walk for days.

"Get. Out!" Maeyve bellowed between pants, snapping me out of my fixation.

Clenching my fists, I stormed out of their suite, slamming the door behind me. If they couldn't keep their hands off each other, I'd have to learn to stop and listen before flying into their room, but I shouldn't have had to in the first place. It didn't appear the king was aware they had mated with each other—not like it was a common thing to find same-sex mated pairs. For whatever reason, he believed Anevae was just clinging to Maeyve as a comfort from the human realm. If they weren't more careful and quiet about their late-night rendezvous, he would find out about their mating and have them separated.

Ultimately, it wasn't my business, so I began the trek back to my room and left them to their activities. But as I walked, more cries of pleasure erupted from their room, and I couldn't help but imagine what would've happened if I accepted Anevae's invitation.

The thought had my cock throbbing to the point of pain, even though I knew there would be consequences.

I needed to find a more meaningful release than just fucking my hand. If I didn't, I wouldn't be able to keep my hands to myself for much longer.

Shoving my door open, I went straight to my wardrobe, where I redressed in my usual black leather pants, tunic, and boots. I hated bulky armor—how it limited my movements and speed—so I stuck to simple clothing, even on duty. Plus, for this excursion, I didn't need to impress anyone; all my clothes would end up on the floor at some point anyway.

Bounding down the stairs, I exited the castle and made my way into Kanlyrae. I weaved through the crowded streets in town until I reached the middle-class area that hid my destination—a brothel I'd been to numerous times since becoming a guard at the castle. Most of the time, I could find a woman who was willing to let me partake in her body on the castle grounds, but that evening, I was desperate to find a release quickly. Easily.

I entered the dimly lit establishment, and one of the courtesans—a fae named Amara—greeted me, "Hiya, Em! Long time no see."

"Nice to see you, Amara," I said as she dropped the cloth she was cleaning with, giving me her full attention.

Huffing out a laugh, she slowly sauntered over to me. "Always so formal, Em. If you want your usual, she's with another client, but I'd be more than happy to help you, too."

When she was directly in front of me, she placed her pale, dainty hand on my chest and looked up into my eyes. Meeting Amara's honey-colored gaze, my heart contracted. As much as I wanted to pull away, I forced myself to stay put. I wanted to get lost in someone, *anyone* else. The fae before me could make me forget Anevae—make me forget that I wanted her, even if only for a while.

But standing there, staring into Amara's eyes, I couldn't help but compare the two. Amara's eyes were warm pools of smooth honey I could easily sink into, while Anevae's were calm blue oceans in which I could get lost and never want to be found.

Shifting my gaze to the rest of Amara's face, her other features seemed muted in comparison to Anevae's. Her lips were thin and dull, her nose short and pointed, her cheekbones hollow and devoid of color. Her mousy blonde hair was short and straight, but Anevae's was a silky mass of long, wavy crimson I could tangle my fingers in.

Compared to Anevae, she was basically skin and bones with such slight curves that she looked nearly straight as a board. Amara's hips were narrow, and her breasts were barely big enough to fit into the palm of my hand. Anevae, on the other hand, was all luscious curves with wide hips and breasts so full I couldn't hold one single-handedly.

Irritation sparked deep in me. I couldn't keep comparing every woman to Anevae. But since I'd laid eyes on her, she was the only woman I could think of. I wanted to be able to touch her every which way I pleased, to bring her pleasure, and to worship her body every day and night as she deserved.

But she hated me. And I'd never be able to have her because I was her bodyguard, and she was a royal. She was a fae, and her grandfather despised anyone who wasn't, even though he trusted us to protect him and his family.

Pulling myself from my thoughts, I looked into Amara's eyes and nodded. Every fiber of my being screamed for me to leave—to change my mind and return to the castle...to Anevae.

But I ignored it and let Amara lead me into one of the private rooms at the back of the establishment. On the occasions I'd visited the brothel, the courtesans knew I liked my privacy even if they hadn't been with me intimately.

When we reached the bed, she turned to me and reached for my shirt, but I stopped her. "Before we start, I need to make something clear. You've seen me around but never been with me, and you don't know what I'm like. When I fuck, I feed too. I can also be very rough. I know you've been here for many years and have likely seen a variety of clients, but I just want to be transparent before we begin. If you're not comfortable, you need to say so now."

As I spoke, her eyes widened slightly, and her heart rate spiked, but I could smell her arousal. She was turned on and scared at the same time.

Had she ever been with a vampire before? If not, this could be so much fun for both of us.

Nodding, she stuttered, "O-okay."

I smirked at her as I took a step closer and reached for the strap of her dress, sliding it down her shoulder. Then, I skimmed my fingers against her skin back up to her neck. Her whole body shook as she shivered under my touch.

Leaning in, I captured her lips with mine, and she moaned softly into my mouth. I slid my hand into her hair and grabbed a handful, yanking on it to expose her neck to me. When I began kissing a trail down her neck, she went rigid, but I continued, enjoying the scent of her fear. She smelled of daisies and honey, an interesting mix I'd never smelled before, but when mixed with fear, it gave it a bitter edge that drove me wild. Fae blood was my favorite—so sweet and fragrant.

I placed a kiss just above her pulse point, then whispered, "Don't worry. I'm not going to feed from you until my cock is buried deep inside your cunt, and everyone can hear you scream."

Her arousal heightened as she sharply inhaled. When she didn't relax, a breathy laugh left my lips, and she trembled. She was terrified, even if she wouldn't admit it. I was loving it. It was exactly what I needed to get my mind off Anevae.

Moving slowly, I placed another gentle kiss against the artery in her neck, feeling it pound under my lips as I reached up with my free hand to slide her other strap off. Her dress fell to the floor, and as with the other courtesans, she wore no undergarments, giving me easy access to her entire body.

Releasing her hair, I trailed kisses to her lips and pushed her back toward the bed. As soon as her knees hit the edge, I lifted her by the ass, pulled her flush against me, and climbed onto the bed. Her arms instantly wrapped around me until we reached the middle, where I slowly lowered her onto the mattress.

Unlocking our lips, I unraveled her arms from around me so I could undress myself. My cock was straining painfully against my trousers, ready to be buried deep inside her. As I set foot on the ground, she raised herself on her elbows to watch me. A grin spread across my face.

If she wanted a show, I'd give her one.

Keeping eye contact with her, I slowly removed each article of clothing. As soon as my cock sprung free of its confinement, her mouth popped open. It was of average length but thicker—women rarely expected that.

With a short laugh, I crawled back up her body, kissing her soft skin each step of the way. When I reached her neck, I wiggled myself between her thighs and asked, "Are you ready?"

She let out a shaky breath, ran her hands up my sides, and panted, "Yes."

I nestled my tip into her entrance, waiting for her to protest. "Are you sure?"

She nodded her head vigorously as she gripped my arms tightly.

In one swift movement, I sunk my cock deep inside of her, and she writhed in pleasure. Giving her no time to adjust to my size, I rocked my hips, pumping in and out of her fast and hard.

"Oh my gods," she cried, throwing her head back as I quickened my pace. She dug her nails into my shoulders and rolled her hips into me, matching my movements and tilting her body just enough that her walls clamped around me tightly. Panting, my climax built as I continued thrusting into her.

As I grew closer, I grazed my elongated fangs against her skin, just above her pulse. She gasped, but then her nails dug into my flesh deeper, drawing blood. The pain fueled my passion, and I struck, biting her neck deeply.

Initially, she clenched against me, trying not to scream, but the pleasure quickly took over, and she was spilling over the edge. When she let loose the scream she held back, her pussy clamped my cock tightly, urging me to climax, but I wasn't ready.

Retracting my fangs, I took a long draw of her sweet blood and moaned. Then, I pounded into her as hard and fast as I could, building my orgasm closer to its peak and not caring if I was hurting her.

When she began gripping my shoulders and moaning again, I could tell another orgasm was building. Continuing my pursuit, I took another long pull of her blood and let my body take over until we were orgasming together.

Lifting my mouth from her neck, I nicked my lip with one of my fangs and gathered a drop of my blood on my tongue to heal the bite on her neck. Her hands fell to the bed, a limp, shaking mess, as she breathed heavily. Withdrawing myself from her, I climbed off the bed to clean myself and get dressed.

Before leaving, I retrieved several coins from my pocket and handed them to her. "Thank you. I'll see myself out."

Chapter Eleven

Anevae

The next morning, I woke up wrapped up in Maeyve's arms. When I peeked my eyes open, the sun shone so brightly through the windows on either side of my bed that I buried my face back into Maeyve's neck to escape it. I'd never been fond of bright lights. Nuzzling in, I placed a kiss on our mating mark and inhaled her sweet scent. The first time I'd walked into her cabin in the human realm, I thought it was just the space that smelled of vanilla and berries, but in reality, it was her.

Closing my eyes, I tried to get comfortable again. I wasn't ready to get up yet—to deal with all of the bullshit I'd gotten myself into coming to Caellaias. But, as I started drifting off, there was a knock on the door. I tried to ignore it, but another more insistent knock came a minute later.

"Go away! I'm trying to sleep," I yelled.

But it was no use. Someone came barging into the room with heels clacking on the wooden floor. "Good morning, Your Highness. You must be up now. It's almost time for your lessons. It would be best if you weren't late," the intruder said in a high-pitched voice as she placed something on the table. Maarya.

Dammit.

Refusing to move, I said, "I've made it very clear that I do not intend to stay here. These lessons are pointless for me to attend. Let's not waste everyone's time. Please leave, Maarya. I'm going back to sleep now."

"I am following your grandfather's orders, and he will not take no for an answer. Your breakfast is waiting for you on the table. I will return in thirty minutes to take you to your lessons," she said, then clapped. "Up and at 'em, Your Highness."

Her heels clacked across the floor, and the door closed behind her.

"For fuck's sake. What doesn't my grandfather understand about me not staying in Caellaias? I guess if I go to these lessons, it'd be great to learn about my magic." With a sigh, I kissed Maeyve's neck and sat up.

Rolling onto her back, she stretched and said, "That's a good way to look at it, but don't hold your breath. You know your grandfather is going to want you to learn about the history."

As I rolled out of bed, I huffed out a laugh. "I think I already know enough to make it back home when it comes time. Anyway, I'm hungry, and Maarya brought us food."

Chuckling, she rubbed her eyes and sat up. "I knew the fastest way to your heart was through your stomach, but damn. Save some for me, please. We both used a lot of calories last night, and I think I filled you up more than you did me—I can be pretty insatiable."

"Excuses, excuses. You better hurry and get out of that bed if you want any. I'm not waiting for you."

She threw off the blankets and jumped out of the massive bed, naked as the day she was born. When she sprinted directly at me, I shrieked and braced for the impact; there was no point in running from her.

She wrapped me in a big bear hug. "You didn't even try. You're no fun."

I giggled and said, "We're both completely naked. It's not like I could've run out of here without showing everything to everyone—which I really don't want to do. There's nowhere in this room I could have run to that you wouldn't have caught me instantly, either."

"I guess you're right."

"I am actually hungry, though. Can we eat, please?" I whined.

"Fine. You're still no fun, though."

When she released me, I kissed her on the cheek and whispered my thanks. Maarya had brought us two plates, each consisting of eggs, some kind of sausage patties, and toast. The plates rested on a platter alongside two glasses of what looked like orange juice.

I grabbed my food and sat on one of the couches while Maeyve sat opposite me. I was caught off guard by the way the eggs were slightly sweeter than the ones I was used to in the human realm. The sausage was also a little chewier, which was a strange texture to me. The toast and orange juice, however, were exactly like the stuff I enjoyed back home, and that was comforting.

After breakfast, I began searching for something to wear for the day. Even though I didn't plan to stay in Caellaias for long, I loved the dresses made for me, and I contemplated taking them home when the time came.

Pulling out a teal summer dress, I threw it on and began my search for a new pair of underwear. When I looked through the armoire the day before, I hadn't seen any undergarments, so I continued searching.

"Is everything okay? What are you looking for?" Maeyve asked as she came up behind me, already fully dressed.

"I'm looking for underwear, but I can't find any. Can you grab me a pair from our bag, please?"

"Sure, but I'd much prefer you not to wear them. Gives me easy access," she said.

Scoffing, I straightened up the armoire and turned back to the bed where Maeyve sat with my requested underwear.

"Thank you. You can't keep ruining them like you did last night. I don't want to walk around without them. It's...uncomfortable," I said.

She let out a soft laugh and helped me finish getting dressed.

After, I wandered to the vanity to brush my hair and asked, "How many more pairs of clothes do you have? If we're here for too much longer, we'll need to find a way to wash them or get you more. It's not like you can wear mine."

"I'm not worried about it right now, love."

"Fine. Let's go," I said as I grabbed her hand, pulling her with me to the door.

When I opened it, I came face to face with Maarya, hand raised, about to knock.

Her face lit up as she met my gaze, "Goodie. You're dressed. Come, come."

"Alright. Let's go. But, just know that if I feel these lessons are unnecessary, I will not continue to attend them."

She crossed her arms and cleared her throat. "Your Highness, with all due respect, you will attend lessons per your grandfather's request. He will *not* take no for an answer. You will also do well not to anger him more than you already have. You did not see the half of it last night. Now, come. You're going to be late."

"I will go *one* day and determine how to proceed."

Shrugging her shoulders, she said, "It's a start. Let's go."

Maeyve and I followed Maarya through the castle into a large room of weapons on tables and racks, ready for use. Mirrors lined one wall, reminding me of a dance studio. On the other side of the room was a man with massive black feathered wings and smooth light-brown skin standing at least half a foot taller than me.

Holy shit. Is this supposed to be my teacher? What the hell is he?

Maarya stopped beside the man and turned back to me. "Your Highness, this is Cassiel. He is the instructor your grandfather has employed to teach you anything you may need to know about the kingdom and your powers."

Cassiel's gaze met mine, and all the air left my lungs. His rounded-almond-shaped eyes were the color of an orletaylaer and so vivid that it was unnerving. He bowed deeply, breaking our eye contact.

When he rose, he wouldn't meet my eyes but addressed me as was expected, "Your Highness, it's a pleasure to serve you."

Still trying to catch my breath, I fumbled over my words, "Um. Th-thank you? You're not really serving me. You're teaching me, right?"

He smiled brightly, spreading his full lips to show off his straight white teeth. "Teaching *is* a service, Your Highness."

"I will leave you all to it! Emrhys will be by to escort you back to your room just before lunch. And Anevae, be nice to the angel. He really is here to help you," Maarya said before she excused herself.

Once she was gone, I said, "Look, I don't plan to be here for long—"

"Your Highness, if you are going to stay in Caellaias for any length of time, there is much you should know. From what I understand, you were raised in the human realm, correct?" Cassiel asked.

"I was," I said, squeezing Maeyve's hand to ground me.

"You are not familiar with this land like someone who was raised here, and right now, you need to learn everything necessary for survival in Caellaias."

"What could I possibly need to know if I don't plan to be here long?" I snipped.

Cassiel's brow rose, and a half-smile graced his lips. "Do you plan to leave Caellaias the same way you came in?"

"I, well, I don't know. I haven't thought about it yet."

"You ought to. If you are not able to find a carriage to transport you back to Maiviraea's portal, you will likely be walking, correct?"

"I guess? But what does that—"

"And what will you do if you run into a keozea?"

Maeyve tensed beside me.

"A what?" I asked, tilting my head to the side.

"A keozea is a bird with sharp teeth lining its massive beak, long, deadly talons, and wings much larger than mine," he said, then cocked an eyebrow at Maeyve.

Clearing her throat, she said, "I haven't been to Caellaias in decades, Cassiel. And, might I mention that the majority of my time was spent in a brothel with minimal schooling? I know many of the creatures outside, but they were the least of my worries—far more dangerous creatures were making their way in for me to conquer."

"It sounds like you may have a lot to learn, too. And I urge you to consider your plans to get back to the human realm before you actually leave. The keozea isn't nearly the most malevolent creature standing between the castle and any of the portals throughout the kingdom."

Chapter Twelve

Emrhys

Of course, Anevae's pet was sitting against the wall of the training room while she was speaking with Cassiel. Angels were always straightforward about everything, so I was sure he'd tell her how Caellaias truly was. They also often believed they were above everyone else, which didn't sit well with me. I wasn't introduced to this one before he was brought in, so I couldn't form a complete opinion about him yet.

I cleared my throat from my spot in the doorway and clasped my hands behind my back. Maeyve was already staring at me as if she could sense me coming from miles away, but Cassiel and Anevae looked up in surprise.

"Is it already lunchtime?" Anevae asked with furrowed brows as she glanced around for a clock.

"I'm afraid it is, and I've come to escort you back to your room, Your Highness. Your meal will be waiting for you there," I said, careful to keep my voice devoid of emotion.

Anevae rolled her eyes. "Thank you, Cassiel. Sounds like I have to head back to my prison. Have a great rest of your day."

She offered a hand for him to shake, but he only stared at her with a puzzled look on his face.

After laughing for a minute, I explained, "It's called a handshake, Cassiel. It's something humans do when greeting or parting."

"Ah. I see," he said, then reached for her hand. As soon as they made contact, he jumped.

She jerked her hand back and said, "I-I'm so sorry. It was a pleasure to meet you. I'll, uh, see you tomorrow, I guess."

Maeyve jumped up from the floor and rushed to Anevae's side. Something was wrong. Anevae's mouth hung open as Maeyve dragged her to the door.

"Move," Maeyve said through gritted teeth as they approached me.

When I didn't move quickly enough for her, her bright orange eyes met mine, and she growled. I snapped out of whatever trance I was in and turned to lead them to their room.

What the fuck was that?

We walked in silence, but Anevae's heartbeat was thudding in my ears at an alarming rate. Again, I fought with myself, wanting to turn around and comfort her—to figure out what was happening. I tried to justify my desires because I was her guard and needed to make sure she was okay. I'd only hoped Maeyve would've said something if she wasn't.

When we reached their room, I instructed them to wait in the hallway for a moment so I could make a quick sweep-through to make sure everything was in order. I would not let myself slack on my duties just because I was drawn to my charge. I took every job I'd been given throughout my career seriously.

As I exited, Maeyve pulled Anevae in and slammed the door in my face. Again.

Damn, mutt.

A chuckle sounded from behind me, and I turned to find Aeros looking smug against the wall.

Scowling at him, I asked, "What's so funny?"

He flashed a sharp-toothed grin. "I just think it's funny how you let the mutt treat you. I know they're mated—I can smell them on each other. But man, would I love to watch them fucking each other into the night. I'm sure that's hot."

My face grew red as I remembered what I'd walked in on the night prior. But the heat creeping up my neck switched from embarrassment to rage.

"Ooooh. You like her too, huh? You want a little bit of that royal pussy?"

"Enough," I hissed.

Throwing up his hands, he shrugged his shoulders. "Hey, all I'm saying is if you get some, don't let the king catch you. You know that won't go over well. He has the whole spiel on 'No intermixing of the territories' and 'Half-breeds are disgusting.' Yet here he is, both of his daughters fell in love with beings that weren't fae, and the two granddaughters he knows about are half-breeds. His family isn't as perfect as he wants it to be, and I wonder how he feels about that."

"Shut the fuck up, Aeros. The royal family's business and how they handle it are none of our concerns. The king will—"

A deep laugh rumbled from his chest. "Do you really think that's the case? Because we're both *personal* guards to the king's *granddaughters* who are *royalty*. We have to look out for them and make sure that nothing happens while they're under our watch. Sure sounds to me like their business has a lot to do with us—"

Eirian's door opened. Her eyes immediately landed on me, and her cheeks went flush. "I-I'm so sorry. I didn't mean to interrupt your conversation."

"Your Highness," I said as I bowed.

Aeros turned to Eirian, bowed deeply, and took her hand to kiss her knuckles. "Your Highness, you did not interrupt anything important. How may I be of service to you this afternoon?"

When Eirian met his gaze, her blush deepened. "I, uh, I would like to go to the garden. But I can wait for a while."

"Nonsense!" Aeros bellowed. "Emrhys, it was a pleasure speaking with you." He gave me a wink and gestured for Eirian to follow him. "I will escort you whenever you are ready, Your Highness."

Rolling my eyes, I positioned myself outside Anevae's door, standing watch for the gods knew what.

Chapter Thirteen

Maeyve

What the hell happened? Are you okay? I asked Anevae through our bond.

She was seated on one of the couches, eyes wide open, staring at the door. I waited a moment for her to respond or acknowledge me, but she didn't move an inch.

Taking a step closer, I waved my hand in front of her face and asked again, *What. The. Hell. Was. That? What happened, Anevae?*

When she answered me, it was in the smallest voice possible that whispered into my thoughts. *Skin-to-skin contact with Cassiel gives me the same tingling feeling as when I touch you or Emrhys. I-I can't have three mates, can I? What is wrong with me? There has to be something wrong with me.*

Shock spread through my body like a tidal wave. *I don't think there's anything wrong with you. I've never heard of that happening before, but I didn't have a lot of formal schooling like others in the kingdom have had. It doesn't mean it hasn't happened before. We'll get to the bottom of it; let's try not to overthink things right now.*

How can I not overthink things, though? I don't know anything about this stuff. My mom told us about the land and the king—that's it. My father never allowed her to tell us anything else and tried to make her sound crazy when she talked about it.

I took a seat beside her on the couch and wrapped her in my arms. She leaned into my embrace and began crying softly. I knew it was all a lot for her—it was a lot for me—but I wanted her to know I wasn't going anywhere.

As I sat there with her, I closed my eyes and took a few deep breaths to at least try to calm myself. So many questions swirled in my mind, but the one that mattered most to me then was if she could have multiple mates. If she did, what would that mean for me? I couldn't handle being kicked to the wayside as someone's last choice again. I'd never be able to give her everything she ever wanted or deserved.

We sat in silence for a while as I rubbed Anevae's back. I was pulled from my racing thoughts when my stomach grumbled. Anevae was still lost in her own mind and crying ever so softly.

Patting her on the back, I said, "Love, we need to eat. Let me grab our plates, okay?"

She pulled away from me and nodded, allowing me to retrieve our food. When I returned, she seemed to have composed herself enough to discuss things. *We need to find someone who can help us process this possibility,* she said through the bond.

I was actually thinking the same thing myself. But we don't know anyone in this castle at this point. What happens if we ask the wrong person for help?

We ate in silence, considering things. When Anevae placed her unfinished plate on the table, she pulled her knees to her chest. *The only person I trust around here is you. I can't even trust my own sister anymore. Maybe I could ask Cassiel about it at my lesson in the morning? He seems very knowledgeable, and I'm sure he felt it, too. Or, I could go out on a limb and ask Emrhys. He's still in the hallway.*

I growled involuntarily at her latter suggestion. *I don't trust that vampire any further than I can throw him, but he would have the quickest answer. How do we know he won't run off and tell the king, though? He tried to kidnap you, and the king trusts him. He's been the king's right-hand man for the gods know how long. As far as asking Cassiel, my biggest concern is that we don't know his alliances. I'm not sure if we should risk it so soon without knowing whether he would immediately report back to your grandfather.*

She rested her head on the back of the couch as she thought about things. When she looked at me, her eyes were bloodshot, and a tear slid down her cheek. *I don't know what the best option is. Part of me wants to act like it didn't even happen. I don't want to be tied to this world any more than I already am. Another mate would mean another attachment…another reason not to leave. If it weren't for my sister, I'd go right now. I almost think I should. Getting her home might be easier with my parents' help, but I worry that my grandfather would send Emrhys after me if we ran.*

Let's take a couple of days to think about this, okay?

After taking a breath, she wiped her eyes and said, *Okay. I need a bath. Would you like to join me?*

I would love to.

Smiling, she took my plate and put it on the table so she could sit on my lap. Caressing my face, she whispered, "I love you. Thank you for everything you do for me every day. And thank you for helping me through things like this. So often, I let myself get in over my head, and I have a hard time seeing a way out."

I wrapped my arms around her and pulled her closer. "Say you love me again. Please?" I whispered back.

She placed her forehead against mine and murmured, "I love you, Maeyve."

I captured her lips with mine as I'd done so many times before. I never wanted to break contact with her because she made me feel whole—she made my life worth living. I'd spend the rest of my life showing her how much she meant to me as long as she'd let me.

I love you too, Anevae. More than you know, I said through the bond.

Pulling back, she broke the kiss and slid off my lap. The separation of our bodies left me wanting more from her. She stepped back and pulled her dress over her head. When she deposited it on the floor, she slid off her panties, and I let my eyes skim over her bare skin, admiring every inch. Even the things she considered imperfections made her beautiful and unique.

When I looked back into her eyes, they were hooded with lust and threatened to consume me—to drown me in their blue depths. My girl would always get what she wanted. All she had to do was take it...or beg hard enough for me to give it to her.

She climbed onto my lap, straddling me, and wrapped her arms around my neck again. With slow, featherlight touches, I brushed my fingertips from the tops of her thighs up to her large, perky breasts. Taking one in each hand, I grazed my thumb across the tight peaks and the jewelry that adorned them, causing her to suck in a sharp breath. Keeping eye contact with her, I lowered my head to suck one of her nipples into my mouth. Her lips parted, and a small moan escaped her as I rolled the flesh and metal across my tongue.

When her eyes began to close, I bit down on her nipple. *Eyes on me, Love.*

Refocusing on me, she tangled her fingers in my hair and ground into me. Her pussy was so wet it soaked through the pants I wore. Liquid heat flowed straight to my clit, making it throb painfully.

As much as I want to be your undoing, I think you may end up being mine.

Letting go of one breast, I smacked her ass. She gave a quiet yelp and gripped my hair tighter.

I huffed out a small laugh and popped off her breast. "Come on, let's get you in the bath. We can continue this afterward."

Chapter Fourteen

Emrhys

Left to my own thoughts and no one to talk to, I paced in front of Anevae's room. There was nothing I could do to get my mind off what happened downstairs between Anevae and Cassiel. All they'd done was shake hands. Cassiel seemed to hold his ground well enough, but Anevae jumped like she'd been shocked. Maybe more of her magic had surfaced when she wasn't expecting it.

I paced and pondered until dinnertime neared and knocked on Anevae's door. She needed to be getting ready, but I hadn't heard any movement inside for over an hour. After waiting for a moment with no answer, I knocked again, listening intently for any movement or verbal response. No one even stirred.

With a frustrated growl, I shoved open the door to find Anevae and Maeyve lying on the bed, completely naked and fast asleep. The sight of them tangled up together brought back flashes of Anevae on top of Maeyve. My cock grew harder the longer I stood there staring at them.

"Fucking hell," I muttered as I readjusted myself before clearing my throat, hoping it was loud enough to wake them. Maeyve stirred first. She untangled herself from Anevae and then stretched before sitting up to look around the room. Her eyes landed on me, and a look of disdain came over her face.

"You really like to come in here at the worst times," she growled. "Get the fuck out of our room. You're not welcome or wanted in here."

Anevae rolled onto her back, rubbed her eyes, and then looked in my direction. As soon as her eyes met mine, she blushed and quickly covered herself.

"What are you doing in here?" she demanded.

I stepped further into the room and closed the door behind me. Leaning against the door, I breathed a laugh. "It's nearly dinnertime. Your grandfather will expect you to join him in the dining hall. If you don't get going soon, you'll be late, and he'll be displeased. You may have only just gotten here, but you're already getting on his nerves. I suggest you stay in his good graces as long as you can."

"Is this seriously going to be an everyday thing?" Anevae asked.

"Yes, so I suggest you get used to it. Now, get up and get dressed. You don't have much time."

Electricity began gathering in the room, making the hair on my arms stand on end.

"You're going to want to learn how to control your powers before you hurt the wrong person," I said.

Her brows furrowed, but the electricity in the room started to fizzle out. "Fine, but if you want me to get dressed, you need to leave."

Chuckling, I didn't move an inch. I enjoyed teasing her. "Are you being shy now, princess? I never would've guessed with that little show you put on for me last night. You even went as far as inviting me to join you guys."

Her cheeks flared red, and she tried to stammer out a response but couldn't. Feeling satisfied, I took my leave so we wouldn't be late. I wasn't lying when I said the king would be displeased if she was late.

After several minutes of slamming armoire doors and things being thrown around, the door flew open. Anevae stomped out of the room, shoving past me, and hissed, "Let's fucking go."

Before Maeyve could exit the room, I grabbed Anevae's arm, pulled her back flush against me, and gripped her throat with my other hand. "I don't like this attitude you're giving me, princess. I'm just trying to help you out," I whispered in her ear. Her pulse kicked against my hand, and the scent of her sweet arousal filled my nostrils. My cock stiffened, pressing into her lower back, and I chuckled. "Mmmm. You like this, do you? Too bad we have to get you to dinner. Maybe after, we can have a little fun, and Maeyve can watch us like I watched you guys last night."

"Get. The. Fuck. Off. Me. I don't care if we're fated to be with each other; you will never be mated to me. Don't count on me ever inviting you into my bed again either," she growled, then stomped down on my foot. When I didn't budge, she did it again. When I still didn't move, she raised her free hand, balled it into a fist, and tried to bring it down on my groin, but I dodged her. Her reflexes were nowhere near as quick as mine, especially with the suppressant still lingering in her system. Even when they fully dissipated, she'd likely never be able to match my speed.

Tsking, I said, "That wasn't very nice, Anevae. Your grandfather won't like your attitude, nor will he tolerate it to the extent I do. So, you might be careful in his presence. Now, fix that attitude, and let's get going before we're late."

Without warning, I let her go, causing her to fall forward. Maeyve rushed forward to catch her before she hit the floor. When our gazes met, her eyes bore into me, orange eyes like an intense fire burning a hole right through me. I couldn't help but laugh as I strolled down the hall toward the stairs and led them to the dining hall.

Dinner went by without incident, and I was grateful for it. Anevae minded her manners with her grandfather as I suggested, and I was invited to join the family at the table for dinner again. Because Aeros was Eirian's guard, he sat beside her, and I was instructed to sit beside Maeyve. The tension rolling off her threatened to drown me.

She was coiled like a spring, ready and defensive of anything that might happen to Anevae. Despite the way she would backtalk me, she was always silent when in the king's presence. What exactly was she afraid of? Maybe it was that the king would send her away or break their bond. Even though he was fully capable of doing so, it was unlikely that he would. Fortunately for Maeyve, he still seemed oblivious to their relationship.

I zoned out for the remainder of dinner. If conversations were happening, they didn't include me. When the king finally excused us, I escorted Anevae and Maeyve back to their room. They were quiet for the whole walk, which I didn't mind. The less I was reminded of what I'd never have, the better.

After they were inside, I waited for their evening guard to relieve me so I could go to my own room. I didn't want to listen to them fucking again because they couldn't keep their hands off each other when they were alone. Even just thinking of them together had my cock aching. I hoped it would get easier to be around them or the king would change my station.

When the night guard got there, I rushed off to my room and tried to push the thoughts of Anevae and her beautiful body out of my head. I didn't want to return to the brothel so soon, but if I walked in on them again, I would probably have to. I wasn't sure how I was going to stay Anevae's guard without something happening between us—whether we wanted it or not.

Chapter Fifteen

Anevae

The next day started very much the same as the day prior. Maarya came flouncing into my room, adamant that Maeyve and I needed to get up. When I tried to protest, she shut me up with a delicious breakfast and promptly left to let us eat and get dressed before escorting us to the training room for my lessons with Cassiel.

When Maeyve and I joined Maarya in the hall, I asked, "Maarya, would it be possible to get some additional clothes made?"

Stopping, she turned to look at me. Her face was pale, and her eyebrows knit tightly together. "Is everything not to your liking, Your Highness?"

I shook my head and answered, "It's not that, Maarya. I'd really like to have some new undergarments and more casual clothing. I can't go around in dresses *all* the time. Also, there aren't any clothes that will fit Maeyve in my armoire. Can we have some clothes made specifically for her as well?"

Relief washed over her face as she let out a long breath. "We can absolutely do that, Your Highness. I will send a tailor up to get measurements for Maeyve this afternoon and put in a request for your additional clothing. However, you will find that most women wear dresses year-round here in Caellaias. And as far as undergarments—well, um. Many beings don't often wear them."

My eyes widened. "Oh, uh. Okay. I would appreciate having at least a few pairs of underwear. I'm not really a fan of going commando. It just doesn't feel...right."

Maarya quirked her head and raised an eyebrow but decided not to ask any questions. Instead, she nodded in understanding before continuing to the training room. When we arrived, she curtsied and excused herself, hurrying off to whatever task she had to complete next.

Walking into the room, an intricate map I hadn't seen the day before covered half of the wall of mirrors. Intrigued, I approached it to get a better look at it.

"Good morning, Your Highness. I'm pleased to see that you have returned."

Spinning in a circle, I searched for Cassiel but couldn't find him. When my gaze returned to the map again, he appeared out of thin air, seated on the floor with wings nowhere in sight. A chuckle rumbled through his chest as I let out a startled gasp.

"Where the hell did you come from? And your wings...where did they go?"

Smiling, he rose to his feet and took a step toward me. "Angels are unique beings. We are able to hide our wings when we want, and we also have our own special powers like many others in the kingdom. Mine happens to be something we like to call conveyance. I see you've taken an interest in the map. I plan to discuss the kingdom as a whole today, and over the next week, we will discuss the beings in each area—"

"I already know all of that."

He crossed his arms and gave me an incredulous look. "Is that so?"

"Yes. My mom used to tell my sister and me stories about Caellaias, except my dad used to try to convince us that they were things my mom made up."

"Interesting... Well, if you think you know everything, are you able to point the territories out to me on a map? And do you know which beings come from which territory?"

"I didn't say I knew everything, Cassiel."

Cassiel's jaw clenched as he considered his next words. "I apologize. I did not intend to insinuate that you know *everything*. I was just trying to test your knowledge."

"It's fine. In regards to territories and where they're located, my mom never had a map she could show us of Caellaias. It's been years since I've heard the story, but from what I recall, Eirvanna, originally the home of the fae, is in the center of the kingdom; Maiviraea, where Maeyve and other shifters are from, is the land to the north; Baeruil, where your kind are from, is to the east; to the south is Lamatorre, which is where Emrhys, a vampire, is from; and to the west is Kaeuil which is the home of the demons."

A wide smile spread across his face. "Excellent job recalling all of that. Let me show you where these places are on the map, and I can explain things in greater detail."

Reaching out his hand, he waited for me to take it. I hesitated but finally went for it. Cassiel's grip tightened, and he about jumped out of his skin at the contact. I was becoming accustomed to it, but I'd noticed the feeling I got from each of them was slightly different. When Maeyve's skin made contact with mine, the tingles I got made me feel like I was being wrapped up in a warm hug. With Emrhys, it was this burning under my skin that made me more aware of everything around me. Cassiel's touch made me feel weightless—like I was flying.

Cassiel shook it off and pulled me along like nothing had ever happened. Behind us, Maeyve made her way toward the corner of the room.

Where are you going? What's wrong, love? I asked through our bond.

I'm still just trying to process some things. Please don't worry about me. I just have a lot on my mind right now.

When Cassiel and I reached the map, Maeyve planted herself on the floor so she could watch the door. She would always be my shadow—my protector from the beginning. I couldn't imagine a life without her.

I reached out to her once more through the bond before my lessons truly started. *I'm here if you need me. I love you, Maeyve. Nothing will change that. Ever. Please always remember that.*

On the map, Cassiel showed me every territory as he'd promised, starting with Eirvanna. "Eirvanna is the most populated territory and contains beings of every race, but fae rarely leave the area."

"Why don't the fae leave?" I asked.

"To be honest, I'm not sure, but I believe it has a lot to do with their comfort here. This is their home and where they're comfortable. Aside from Maiviraea, this is the only territory that doesn't get the extreme temperatures some of the others do."

"Oh, well, that makes sense. I assume the capital is Kanlyrae since it's so close to the castle, right?"

"It's not actually. The capital of Eirvanna is Feraetheam, which is more toward the center of Eirvanna than the castle is."

Next, Cassiel spoke about his home, Baeruil. "On the coast is a grand palace that houses the elders—the wisest angels that are centuries old—and other influential figures. It's actually where I grew up. I still have my own quarters in the palace to this day."

"Were your parents elders?"

Cassiel's lips turned down. "They weren't. The elders took me in when I was a child and took very good care of me. But that happened long ago." After clearing his throat, he pointed to another city about twenty miles from the palace. "This is the capital, Haelian, which is where most angels are born."

Moving on, he spoke about Lamatorre—Emrhys' home. Their capital, Ellaenea, was in the south of the territory. He pointed at the northern part of the territory and said, "Up here, there are miles upon miles of hollowed-out trees that act as homes to numerous creatures, but that is a lesson for another day."

"Damn. Now you've got me intrigued. Are they dangerous creatures?"

"Very dangerous. I don't have enough time to discuss them today, so let's keep moving."

When he spoke about Kaeuil, his voice dripped with venom. "Kaeuil is the home of the demons—the natural-born enemies of the angels. Their capital, which really isn't much of one, is Tyrkenea."

As Cassiel explained how barren and hot the land was, I remembered my mom telling me that Kaeuil was similar to how humans thought Hell would be. I let out a small chuckle, but of course, I couldn't tell Cassiel about it because he wouldn't understand.

"Now, I saved the most complex territory for last—Maiviraea," Cassiel said.

"The way my mom explained it to me when I was little was like 'its own little version of Caellaias' in a sense."

"That's actually an interesting way to look at it. It's true that the east and the west are similar in nature to Baeruil and Kaeuil, but the southern piece of the land is the most similar to Eirvanna. The north is another story."

"Okay. I know the east is closest to Baeruil as it shares a border. The...Kolathus, right?" I asked, and he nodded before I continued, "Mountains run along the border. The upper peaks are covered in snow, just like Baeruil. But as you go further down, it becomes more forested. That's about where Maeyve and I entered Caellaias from the portal near my cabin in the human realm."

"That's correct."

"Great. And the western part of the territory shares a border with Kaeuil, so this area has an intense heat and arid climate."

"That is also correct. To the south, Maiviraea is bordered by Eirvanna. It's covered in lush green grass and zyelvris trees; it's a very beautiful area. But, to the north, the territory is bordered by the sea. It's very humid and covered in sand."

"Interesting. Reminds me of Florida." One of Cassiel's eyebrows rose, and he tilted his head, which made me laugh. "It's one of the states in America, back in the human realm. It's hot and humid there all the time. The only good place in that state to me is the beaches, so that's what I associate the state with, I guess."

Cassiel nodded slowly as if trying to understand but was having a hard time doing so. "Anyway. Each piece of the territory has its own capital. The capital of the north is Rilias; to the east is Diathem; in the south is Ceraias; in the west is Dirsethik. I suppose we should stop there. It's almost time for your guard to retrieve you for lunch."

"Already? The lessons today went by so fast."

"That they did."

"Maeyve!" I said and gestured for her to join us.

What is it, my love? she asked before getting up.

It's almost time to go, sweetheart.

With a heavy sigh, she made her way to me. I reached out for her, and when our hands connected, the bond was satisfied, making us both smile.

"Are you two mated?" Cassiel asked.

I continued gazing into Maeyve's mesmerizing eyes as I considered whether I should answer. In the end, I did. "Yes, we are."

"I didn't think beings of the same sex could mate. I've never seen it in my lifetime, and there has never been a case documented that I've come across," Cassiel said and paused momentarily, hesitating to ask his next question. "What do you feel when you touch each other?"

Maeyve looked at Cassiel with an eyebrow raised and went on the defense. "Why do you want to know?"

A blush crept up his cheeks before he answered, "I've heard that it can feel like a spark or like a tingling feeling that travels throughout the body when someone touches their fated mate. Is that what you feel?"

Maeyve's eyes narrowed. "Yes. That's almost exactly what it feels like when we make skin contact."

Trying to comfort her, I squeezed her hand. "I think I know where you're going with this, Cassiel. Is it...possible for someone to have more than one fated mate?"

"It's been rumored that it is possible, but I've never heard of it actually happening," he said.

Taking a deep breath, I bit my lip piercing. Meeting Cassiel's gaze, I held my free hand out and whispered, "Touch my hand and tell me what you feel."

Hesitantly, he did as I asked. As soon as our hands made contact, his eyes widened. "There's no way. It must be part of your powers."

"I don't think that's it. Look, I don't know you very well, so I'm not sure whether I should trust you, but you're very knowledgeable, and I have this gut feeling you can help me make sense of this—especially if you're part of it."

Pulling his hand from mine, he crossed his arms over his chest. "You've piqued my interest."

I looked to Maeyve, hoping she'd either agree or disagree with me, but she just shrugged her shoulders. After a long, shaky breath, I told him everything about my connection with Maeyve and Emrhys, as well as my suspicions after meeting Cassiel himself. "Since my powers have awakened, this hasn't happened when I've made contact with my grandfather or sister. I'm sure if I tried to touch Maarya, Azure, or Acros, they wouldn't feel anything either."

Cassiel was stunned into silence. Then, he gasped, gave me a quick bow, and muttered, "I must go. I will see you tomorrow morning." Then, he disappeared into thin air.

Chapter Sixteen

Cassiel

*I*t can't be.

I'm an angel.

I can't have a fated mate; at least, that's what I've been told my entire life.

Safely back in my room, I rushed to grab my robes so I could go back to Baeruil for the remainder of the day. I needed to do some investigating, but I couldn't find the answers I sought in Castle Rilvara.

When I was in school many, many years before, a seer had told us about one of the first prophecies ever to have been recorded. It spoke of a woman from an unknown territory who would unite the kingdom after eons of turmoil. The prophecy claimed the woman would have mates from all five of the territories. If the prophecy spoke of Anevae, she'd already found her mates from Lamatorre and either Maiviraea or Kaeuil. Could I really be her mate from Baeruil?

After I got dressed, I used my power of conveyance once more to get me to my quarters inside the palace of Baeruil. The moment my feet hit the ground, I shoved the door to my room open and rushed to the library. Every ancient text from the beginning of time was kept in Baeruil's library under the ever-watchful eye of The Librarian.

When I rounded the last corner, the doors to the library came into view. They were crafted using a lightweight but sturdy white stone called gaellian, carved to look like two massive angel wings. As I approached, I admired the elaborate details that had been etched into the stone and accented with glittery gold paint. They were beautiful, but they reminded me just how much of an outsider I was in my own home.

After taking a deep breath, I opened the door and stepped in. The sun's setting rays illuminated the room in orange, streaming in through an entire wall of windows to my right. Numerous tables and chairs were situated beside the wall, allowing those sitting there to enjoy the warmth provided by the sun, even through the windows. The remainder of the room was filled with rows and rows of bookshelves—made from zyelvris trees and another species that died out long before my birth—that reached for the golden ceiling at least a hundred feet above. The rows stretched across the entirety of the massive room, which seemed like miles, but between them, on the other side of the room, the sun glinted off tiny shards of stained glass pieced together to make a mural of a faceless angel. He was said to be the first of our kind, but no one knew his name or what he looked like exactly. The floor below was tiled with more gaellian, polished to a perfect shine.

The Librarian appeared before me as soon as the door closed. She was a short, frail-looking elderly angel with small, white wings. Her white hair was always tied up in a bun, so I never knew how long it was, but it was always pristine—never a hair out of place. Under her barely visible eyebrows were her downturned eyes. They were the most intense ice blue I'd ever seen, and they unnerved me. It wouldn't have surprised me if she could see down to the depths of someone's soul.

Because of her appearance, most underestimated her, but she'd lived for thousands of years, making her one of the oldest angels alive.

In a quiet, shaky voice, she greeted me, "Cassiel, what a nice surprise. You haven't come to visit in quite some time. What brings you to my library today?"

"I have come in search of a prophecy. It's one I have no doubt you know well." Any prophecy that had been reported across the kingdom was transcribed and placed under the protection of The Librarian. Because she watched over them and loved reading them, she knew almost all of them like the back of her hand.

Her eyes lit with excitement, happy to be discussing something so intimate to her. "I am intrigued to hear which prophecy you seek."

"I am in search of the one that speaks of a woman who will unite the kingdom."

"Ah, that one. As you know, we don't have much about it. The prophecy was told many, many years before I was appointed to this position, but let's see what we can find for you."

She led me to a cage across the library, filled to the brim with many of the ancient texts she'd acquired over the years. Conveyance couldn't be used within the palace unless the angel was inside their private quarters or the entrance hall, so no one could enter the cage without first obtaining the key, which The Librarian kept around her neck.

Pulling the key from her neck, she continued, "It's said that one of the first seers in the land was the one to have this vision centuries ago—long before you or even I were born. Although many have tried, it's never been fully transcribed from the ancient language. Not many are familiar enough with the language to make any further attempts. Even I have become rusty with my skills and cannot decipher it."

When we reached the shelf, she skimmed her hand across the spines of several tomes before she slid one off the shelf and placed it into my hands. "This contains the prophecy you seek. Please return it to me in one piece."

"Th-thank you. Would you like it to remain in the library while I look through it?"

"Cassiel, there's only one reason you'd be looking for that prophecy in particular. You cannot learn all that is needed while only looking through it here. You must take it with you to get all the necessary information, especially because it is not fully translated. Please. Take it. And be careful."

I gave her my thanks before retreating to my quarters and returning to the room provided to me in Castle Rilvara. I hadn't expected it to be so easy to get the prophecy from her. I also expected her to want to keep it in the library, but it seemed she may have known something I didn't at the time.

But I wasted little time asking questions I couldn't answer, changing into comfortable clothing, and getting to work.

Chapter Seventeen

Anevae

The following week was much of the same: wake up, breakfast, lessons, lunch, stuck in my room, then dinner. My grandfather kept Eiri and me so busy that we hardly saw each other, let alone talked. I missed my sister, even though she'd betrayed me.

When Emrhys was escorting Maeyve and me back to our room for lunch one day, I stopped in the hall and longingly looked at Eiri's door, where Aeros stood guard. I still hadn't interacted with him much, but he seemed overly full of himself.

Meeting his gaze, I said, "I need to talk to her. I miss her."

A smirk appeared on Aeros' face as he raised an eyebrow at me. "Do you really think that's such a good idea? You nearly unleashed your powers the last time you were left alone with her. I still don't think she's over that."

Standing tall, I met his fierce, frightening gaze straight on. "I don't care if you think it's a good idea or not, and I sure as shit don't give a fuck what you think about me. I wish to speak with her. Regardless of what's happened these last few weeks, she's still my sister. We're both big girls and can speak our own damn minds. Now, move Aeros."

Crossing his arms over his chest, he chuckled as I stared him down. When he didn't move, I sidestepped around him and knocked on the door. Moments later, the door swung open, and I caught a glimpse of the cheerful, upbeat woman who seemed to have disappeared when she came to Caellaias.

Placing my hand on the door to keep her from closing it on me, I blurted out, "Eiri, can we talk, please?"

"Before you try to 'persuade' me again, I am not going home—so stop asking. I love it here. I feel like I'm somewhere I belong for once. But you're too worried about yourself to see any of that. If you're so antsy to go back to the human realm, go. Just keep in mind what Grandfather might do if you run." Then, when my hand slacked, she slammed the door shut in my face.

"Dammit! Eirian, I just want to talk to you!" I yelled, hitting the door once before Maeyve grabbed my hand and pulled me across the hall to our room.

Once the door was shut, tears threatened to fall, but I kept them at bay; she couldn't win this battle—I wouldn't let her. "Why won't she just fucking talk to me? I know she doesn't want to go home, and I'm trying like hell to understand why, but she's got to give me something to work with. I know my grandfather is up to something, but I still don't know what. Eiri hasn't even told me why she came to Caellaias in the first place. I still don't know enough about this place or our grandfather to feel comfortable in the slightest. All Cassiel has taught me thus far is the fucking history and more about the geography. I don't care to know about any of it. I want to fucking go home, but I'm staying here for her, and she's being an ungrateful little brat!"

Stopping next to the bed, a single tear dropped to the floor. I refused to let myself break down, so instead, I flopped onto the bed face first and screamed at the top of my lungs.

The door flung open, and in came a panicked Emrhys. "Is everything okay?"

I scrambled off the bed and stalked toward him, yelling at the top of my lungs, "No! Everything is not fucking okay, Emrhys! I'm stuck in this place I know very little about; my bratty little sister won't talk to me, and I want to go home. Oh, and I have this fucking magic I know absolutely nothing about. It's been a fucking week, and all Cassiel has taught me about is the fucking kingdom, which I have no desire to learn any more about." By the time I was done yelling at him, I was about a foot away and breathing heavily.

Emrhys sighed. "I understand why you're frustrated. This is all new to you, and I can't imagine how you're feeling right now. I know how close you and your sister were, but things have changed. You heard her out there; she's found somewhere she's comfortable and happy. She's finally putting her foot down and standing up for herself. Let her do her thing—if she needs you, she'll tell you—but give her some space. As far as the angel, I'm sure he's teaching you what he believes is important. He will teach you about your magic, but you need to learn to control your anger in the meantime."

As I stood there, eyes locked on Emrhys, Maeyve came up next to me and grabbed my hand. She hissed at the contact, my magic shocking her, but she didn't let go, and her calming ability washed over me.

"I wish you wouldn't do that," I whispered. "He has a point. I need to learn how to control my anger, which may help me control my magic. If you keep stepping in to calm me down, I can't learn how to calm myself on my own."

Maeyve squeezed our intertwined hands and pulled me into her embrace. My eyes remained on Emrhys. A flash of jealousy crossed his face as Maeyve tightened her grip, but it was gone in an instant. When I arrived at the castle, he'd told me he never thought he'd find his fated mate. Since he'd found me, I wondered how hard it was for him to watch me be intimate and comfortable with another. The answer to my question came when he lowered his eyes to the floor and excused himself, returning to the hall.

Pulling back from Maeyve's embrace, I sighed. *I know I should hate him, but it's becoming more and more difficult as time goes on.*

I'm sorry, my love. Now that the suppressant is leaving your body, it may become more difficult to deny your mate bond with him and Cassiel. I think that's why it was so hard for me to leave you alone after you moved into your cabin.

I gasped. *That's why I sought you out so desperately the day I came to your cabin to introduce myself. I usually hate being social, and that day, I couldn't get the possibility of meeting you out of my mind. I didn't want to finish the greenhouse or be alone in my cabin. My soul knew you were out there—so close—and it led me right to you.*

Leaning in, Maeyve gave me a passionate kiss. When she pulled back, she whispered, "I love you. And I'm so glad you found me that day. I wouldn't have had the courage you did. I spent hours every day outside your cabin watching you, but I didn't want to risk anything. You came to me, and I'll forever be grateful."

Chapter Eighteen

Emrhys

I needed to find a way to control my feelings toward Anevae. I knew I'd never get to be with her, to truly feel a mate bond, but that didn't make it any easier to see her with Maeyve.

When I stepped back into the hall, Aeros looked back and forth between me and the door I'd just stepped through, brows furrowed. "Is everything alright in there, or should we be prepared for all hell to break loose?"

"Worry about your charge, and I'll worry about mine. Now, shut the fuck up," I growled.

Aeros let out a deep chuckle, which was really starting to irritate me. He seemed to think everything was funny in one way or another. Crossing his arms, he leaned against the wall outside Eirian's door. "I *am* worrying about my charge. Yours needs to learn to keep her temper in check. If she doesn't, bad things are going to happen. What the fuck is that angel even teaching her?"

"She has a lot to learn about Caellaias. She didn't have the luxury of growing up in this world like we did. She's doing great, all things considered."

Scoffing, he gestured toward Eirian's door. "This one seems to be picking everything up just fine."

"Eirian has a lot going for her that her sister doesn't. She's had far more exposure to Caellaias, the suppressant Cordilaen was using on the girls has been out of her system for months, and she's a lot more docile and meek than her sister. She wants to please the king with everything she does. Anevae's first encounter with Caellaias was when she arrived with Maeyve a little over a week ago; she's had a more recent dose of the suppressant and doesn't care what her grandfather thinks—she walks to the beat of her own drum."

"Excuses, excuses, Emmy."

"They're facts. And don't call me that."

"Aww. Did I strike another nerve? Such a sensitive vampire. I thought you guys were all macho and mighty."

"Think what you'd like, Aeros. I never believed you dragon shifters could be such fucking assholes, but I was warned, I guess."

Another chuckle rumbled through his chest. "Fine, fine. I'll leave you alone. You'd better keep an eye on her, though. If she's not careful, she won't be able to control her magic, and someone will get hurt. It sure as shit won't be me or Eirian if I can help it."

After that, we stood silently in the hallway, avoiding acknowledging each other. When dinnertime approached, we turned to retrieve our charges. Eirian responded to Aeros almost instantly, telling him she was nearly ready and would be out in a few minutes. But when I knocked on the door to retrieve Anevae and Maeyve, there wasn't an answer.

Of fucking course.

If there was one thing I could guarantee, it was that these two women were always wrapped up in one another. I'd heard it could happen with newly mated pairs, but I'd never seen it firsthand.

Before opening the door, I knocked one more time.

"Give me a fucking second!" Maeyve yelled.

Aeros let out his usual chuckle, but I ignored him. A couple of minutes later, Maeyve opened the door, dressed in some of the new clothing Anevae had requested for her. The black dress hugged her curves, and the low neckline revealed the swells of her breasts. I couldn't deny that the woman was beautiful, but I couldn't stand the way she acted toward me.

"My eyes are up here, Emrhys," she snapped.

Blinking a few times, I said, "I, uh, I know. Where's Anevae?"

"She's almost ready. We'll be out in a few minutes." Then, she slammed the door in my face. I had a feeling she enjoyed doing that.

Huffing, I turned around to find Aeros shaking his head. He tried to hide the smirk that was attempting to grace his lips but failed miserably. A few moments later, just as promised, Anevae and Maeyve came out of their room. Eirian followed suit, emerging from hers shortly after.

"Splendid! Let's get going," Aeros said, turning to take the lead down to the dining hall. He seemed a little too carefree, considering his concerns about Anevae and her sister. The fact he wasn't watching over his charge directly led me to believe he didn't worry about Eirian as much as he claimed.

On the way down, I trailed the group so we could provide protection from both fronts. Much to my relief, Anevae didn't attempt to speak with her sister during the walk. We didn't have far to go, but it gave me hope that she had actually taken my advice.

When we reached the dining room, the women took their usual spots at the table after the king greeted them.

"Emrhys, Aeros, please sit," the king said, gesturing to our newly assigned seats. Since we'd become personal guards to his granddaughters, we'd been invited to join them for dinner every night, but we didn't dare sit until the king instructed us to do so. Once we were seated, the king clapped his hands, and dinner was served.

When the first course was completed, the king turned his attention to Eirian. "My sweet granddaughter. How have your lessons been with Ruelle?"

"Oh, Grandfather, they've been wonderful! I've learned so much from her. I've begun learning even more about my magic and how to control it to the best of my ability over the last few days."

"That's wonderful! I'm very proud of you. Soon, you will be an expert." Then, he turned his attention to Anevae. "How have your lessons been, sweetheart? Have they been to your liking thus far?"

Anevae dropped her fork on her plate with a loud clang and rolled her eyes. "I told you not to bother with the lessons. All Cassiel has taught me is more of the history and geography I hadn't known. I don't plan to stay here, so I don't know why he's so focused on that. I still don't know a thing about my magic, except my damn temper keeps bringing it to the surface."

The king reached out to grab Anevae's hand, making her lip curl. He ignored her reaction and said, "My darling. You must learn about our history. It's a huge part of how we became who we are. But I shall discuss your desire to learn more about your magic with Cassiel. I'd also be happy to assist you in any way I can since you did inherit my powers."

Scoffing, she pulled her hand free from her grandfather's grip. "I'd rather not have to spend more time with you. Once I discover what you've told Eiri to make her forget everything our mom told us growing up, I'll be leaving Caellaias, and I hope I never have to see your face again."

Fury burned in the king's luminous yellow eyes. "You little bitch. You're just like your fucking mother. Everything I've done for you since you arrived, and you still treat me like this. I've even allowed your mutt to stay in the same room as you so she can provide you with some comfort in a new place. You will be staying here, in Caellaias, whether you like it or not. If you try to return 'home,' I will send Emrhys after you, and he will bring you back. This is your home now. You don't belong in the human realm. You are my granddaughter—a royal fae—whether you like it or not. Finish your dinner, and then I want you to return to your room; consider what you have just said to me. I haven't even begun to show you how cruel I can be, but if you keep up, you will not enjoy the consequences."

Snapping his fingers, the servants rounded up the dirty plates, and another set returned with the next course. When the servants exited, Anevae shoved her chair back and stood. Electricity poured from around her as her anger rose.

"Watch yourself, Anevae. Like I said before, those powers are the ones you inherited from me. Now, sit down and eat your dinner."

"I've had my fill and will be returning to my room. Good fucking night," she said through gritted teeth.

Lifting my cup, I gulped down the last bit of blood and stood to escort her to her bedroom.

Chapter Nineteen

Anevae

"**W**hat the fuck is your problem?" Emrhys hissed as he caught up to me.

Stopping, I whipped around to face him. "What's *MY* fucking problem? You heard him in there. He's keeping me here against my will. If he thinks he can force me to stay, he's got another thing coming. He will not stop me from going home, and neither will you."

"You have no idea the lengths he will go to keep you here. If you leave again, he will send me after you. And if *I* don't go after you, he'll send a shifter specializing in tracking, and they will *not* be as gentle as I am. Do you really want that? You have no clue what he's done to try to find your mother. Unfortunately for him, she has glamour magic and is good with it. From what I've heard, she's better than anyone else who has ever been able to wield it. We don't know exactly what magic or other abilities you have yet. Just...stop fighting him so much, if not for anyone but yourself."

Frustrated, I grunted and stomped off to the stairs. But before I could begin the ascent, Emrhys appeared in front of me.

"Damn it, Emrhys. Move! I want to be alone right now."

"Anevae, please," he said as he reached for me. I took a step back and crossed my arms. He frowned, and his voice was pleading as he said, "I'm begging you to be careful when it comes to your grandfather. He's very old; with that comes immense power and numerous connections around the kingdom. He's used to getting his way in every situation. Your grandfather doesn't care who you are; he won't hesitate for a second to make your life a living hell. Next time you see your mother, ask her what he put her through."

"Like you even care about what happens to me."

"Is that really what you think? Because that's nowhere near true. No matter how much you hate it, we're fated to each other. I cannot bear the thought of something—*anything*—happening to you. And if it happened under my watch, I would blame myself for the rest of my miserable life. We both may wish we weren't fated for our own reasons, but there's nothing we can do at this point. I am sworn to protect you, and I will do so with my life because, whether you like it or not, you're mine. I'll do anything imaginable to make sure I'm never separated from you because I can't live without you."

Footsteps echoed down the hallway from the dining hall. I knew, without a doubt, that it was Maeyve coming to look for me.

Emrhys dropped his gaze to the floor and sighed. Stepping aside, he said, "Please just be careful, Anevae."

Without a second glance at him, I stormed up the stairs. My heart was beating rapidly, and my thoughts swirled, thinking about everything he'd just admitted to me.

Damn it! Why does he do this to me?

When I reached my room, I threw the door open and flopped onto my bed again. I wanted to go home and act like none of this had happened. I wanted to pretend that everything about Caellaias was just a dream. The only piece of the 'dream' I wanted to keep was Maeyve.

But then my mind wandered back to Emrhys. Before I rushed upstairs, he'd basically professed his love to me. I was developing such a soft spot for him. Just the thought of being near him made my heart pitter-patter like a little schoolgirl who had a crush on someone she knew she shouldn't have. Was he really going to be the reason I stayed? Then there was Cassiel and the way he made me feel, too. Even though that connection was extremely new, he made me feel important.

Maeyve entered our room, slammed the door shut behind her, and came to sit beside me on the bed. I lay there with my head running a million miles a minute, wondering where to go from there. She didn't ask any questions; she just began stroking my hair.

Why?

Why me?

Why couldn't I be normal?

Why did I have three others attached to me?

When the tears began to fall, I allowed myself a few minutes to wallow. I wouldn't let that horrible man downstairs break me any more than he already had. Then, I pulled myself together and got ready for bed.

Chapter Twenty

Cassiel

News of Anevae's disrespect to the king traveled fast through the castle. She was feisty, and he was livid at her blatant disregard for his title. I'd heard stories about her mother's behavior before she left Castle Rilvara, and it seemed her daughter had her spirit. It was a good thing; she'd need it if she were going to stand up to her grandfather and fulfill the prophecy—if it was actually about her. I still hadn't figured that out yet.

The next morning, she reported to her lessons with Maeyve per usual, and I greeted them, "Good morning, Anevae, Maeyve."

"What about the land am I going to learn today?" Anevae grumbled, rolling her eyes. It seemed the interaction with her grandfather had gotten under her skin.

"You're in a lovely mood this morning. I've actually been informed of your desire to learn about your magic, so we are switching gears to that today."

Secretly, I was excited to see what she was capable of; I'd heard she was already powerful, even with the suppressants still lingering in her system. The ire she felt toward her grandfather and the situation she was in likely contributed to her heightened abilities, but it would be helpful for the lessons to come.

Her beautiful blue eyes lit up as her gaze rose to meet mine. "Really? I'm amazed my grandfather listened to me, especially with as much as I backtalk him. I'm dying to learn how to control my magic and stop these stupid outbursts I keep having."

"You won't be able to learn everything in one day, but that will certainly come with time. Also, please keep in mind that it's going to be a very taxing day. I want to see what you are capable of—I've already heard a lot about what you managed in the gardens. Your mother's magic was reportedly very powerful, so it doesn't surprise me that you seem to be as well. At some point, I'd like to tap in and see if there's anything else you can do—like awaken your wolf. I'd be shocked if you're not able to shift, considering who your parents are."

A wide smile appeared on her lips, and it warmed my soul to see her finally be happy amid so much turmoil. In the past few weeks, I'd only seen her smile a handful of times. Being here made her miserable, and I was finally able to bring her a moment of joy.

Maeyve cleared her throat, ruining the moment. "I feel like I should be the one to teach her about shifting as I myself can do it, too."

"I have no qualms with you teaching her how to shift, but I'd like to see what else she's capable of before we get to that. We know she has electrokinesis, but glamour magic can be more complex to harness."

Both women nodded, and I directed them to their designated spots—Anevae in the middle of the room and Maeyve close but out of danger. Once they were clear on their stations, I set up a few extra targets, trying to avoid the mirrors. Even though her magic couldn't break the glass, I always liked to err on the side of caution.

When I returned to Anevae's side, I took a few steps back and began, "Okay, Anevae, I want you to focus on all the pent-up anger you have, but don't let too much in at once."

She closed her eyes, and her energy filled the room within seconds, making the hair on my arms stand on end. Tendrils of lightning began swirling from her hands after, and her breaths grew ragged.

"That's good, just calm your breathing...that's it, right there. Now, keep hold of that and open your eyes."

Her eyelids fluttered open, revealing a crackling yellow ring around her irises.

As her eyes focused on me, I said, "You're doing great. Don't let the magic consume you, though. Maeyve and I are right here. We won't let anything happen to you." Not daring to break eye contact with her, I pointed toward the open wall where I'd positioned several targets for her to practice throwing her magic at. "I want you to try to direct a ball of energy at each target I've placed along the wall. It doesn't matter if you hit them; I just want to see how well you can harness the magic you possess."

She sucked in a deep breath and focused on one of the targets. Lifting her hand, electricity funneled into her palm and formed a swirling sphere that filled her hand. Then, she cocked her hand back and threw it at one of the targets, hitting damn near close to the bullseye. Once she was comfortable with conjuring balls of energy, she wasted no time, throwing ball after ball toward the targets. Pride welled up inside of me as she hit every single one. Several hits weren't in vital spots, but she hit them nonetheless. It was an incredible feat for someone just learning to control their magic.

When she hit the final target, she lowered her hands.

"Th-that was amazing. I've never seen anyone harness their magic so well on the first try! Let's stop there for now. How did that feel?"

She gave me a weak smile but didn't answer, so I took a few steps closer. The energy continued to crackle around her, and the closer I got, the more it poured off of her. I couldn't understand how she was still going. She kept her eyes locked on me, and while she wasn't standing in a defensive position, the tension in her body was evident. As I got closer to her, the light in her eyes began to fade, and the tendrils of lightning fizzled.

"Shit," I muttered.

"What's wrong?" Maeyve asked, worry creeping into her voice.

"She did too much," I said.

When I was a couple of steps away, the lightning dissipated completely, and her eyes fluttered closed. I caught her just before she hit the ground and lifted her into my arms.

"We need to get her to your room."

Chapter Twenty-One

Maeyve

"What do you mean?" I asked as I rushed up to where Cassiel held a limp Anevae in his arms.

After letting out a nervous laugh, he said, "She...overexerted herself. This is the first time she's truly harnessed her powers. She did go overboard, though, throwing all those energy balls one after the other without giving herself a break in between."

"And you didn't think telling her to pace herself was important? For fuck's sake. Some kind of teacher you are. Give her to me."

He readjusted Anevae in his arms, holding her closer, and glared at me. "I will carry her. Now, take me to your suite, or I will take her to mine."

"You're impossible, too. Fuck," I mumbled with a grunt.

Turning on my heel, I stomped out of the training room and led him upstairs to our suite, not wanting to contemplate being away from her. When we got inside, he laid Anevae down gently on the bed and stepped back, just watching her. I climbed on the bed to sit next to her.

When I settled, I stroked her hair. She looked so peaceful when she slept—a small mercy, everything considered. Over the last few weeks, she'd been so tense, dealing with things she wasn't prepared for because her parents had kept so many secrets from their daughters. Cordilaen and Roarc could've prevented so much if they'd just readied the girls for the day the king found them. They should've known they couldn't keep the world they came from hidden forever.

Cassiel shifted, and I glanced up at him. He'd already been staring at her in a way I didn't like, and then he leaned over and brushed a strand of hair away from her face. That familiar ache of insecurity returned to my chest. Polyamory was common in Caellaias—and I wasn't against it—but I was protective of her and our relationship.

Just as Cassiel stepped back from the bed, the door flew open behind him. The growl that rumbled through the room alerted me to who it was a second before his scent enveloped me—Emrhys.

"What the fuck happened? Is she okay?" he asked frantically as he rushed toward the bed.

"She's fine; she just overexerted herself during training today," Cassiel said nonchalantly.

I shot him a sharp look. He was making it sound like it was no big deal, but I certainly thought it was.

"Wait. You actually let her harness her powers? Already? You've only just begun teaching her about them!" Emrhys' gaze was fixed on Cassiel, eyes pulsing a deep red as he clenched his jaw so tight he'd have likely broken teeth if he was a human.

Cassiel stood his ground and met the vampire head-on. "We had things under control, and she wasn't in any danger with Maeyve and me close by. She just needs to rest for a little while. What we did today was just a test to see what she was capable of. I still don't know to the full extent; we've just scratched the surface. She's more powerful than I ever could have imagined."

When he looked back at Anevae, there was a look of longing in his eyes, like he'd found the answer to every one of his prayers, but it was just out of reach. He was already developing feelings for her.

Gods fucking damn it!

Without meaning to, a snarl reverberated deep in my chest.

Emrhys crossed his arms and turned to me with a look of pure annoyance. "You've got to be fucking kidding me. You feel threatened by this big ol' softie? *You* are mated to her, not me, and definitely not the angel here. They don't have fated mates."

"Don't speak about something you don't know, Emrhys," I said harshly.

His face contorted in confusion as he looked between Cassiel and me. "No. Fucking. Way. Two fated mates are unheard of. Three? That's insane—impossible. There has to be another explanation."

Cassiel cleared his throat and fidgeted with his hands. "I'm still doing research, so I won't say anything is definite yet, but I might've found the reason she could have multiple fated mates, including one of the same sex."

Emrhys's eyes blazed red again as he glared at Cassiel. "I need you to elaborate."

Cassiel sighed. "Did you not just hear me? I can't yet. I don't want to get anyone's hopes up. I also don't want to tell her and have her be disappointed if it's not what I think it is."

"Oh, you can, and you fucking will share everything with us," Emrhys said as he took a step closer to Cassiel.

Cassiel didn't even flinch. "No, Emrhys. I will not. You need to calm down."

Jumping to my feet, I separated the men before they could cause more trouble. "That's enough. Go sit down—both of you—and chill the fuck out. We're all here for her. I don't think she'll be waking up for a bit."

"You're right. I'm going to grab some things from my room. I'll be right back." Cassiel said, and then he disappeared.

"What the fuck?" I said in exasperation.

"He has the power of conveyance. Many of the angels do. Sounds like a pretty cool power if you ask me," Emrhys said as he turned toward the couch.

"No one did ask you, so shut the fuck up."

He bellowed out a laugh as he plopped down on one of the couches close to the fireplace, still keeping a sharp eye on Anevae.

"Aren't you supposed to be in the hallway or something?" I asked.

"As long as I'm guarding her, I can be wherever I'd like...or she'd like."

He wiggled his eyebrows, taunting me, and I fell right into his trap, growling at him just as Cassiel reappeared in the room.

He glanced between the two of us and said, "Unbelievable. I was gone for a couple of minutes, and I return to find you two behaving like children. Knock it off! If Anevae wakes up to this, it's only going to work her up and bring her magic to the surface again. She needs rest, so shut up and sit down."

Emrhys and I were locked in a staring match for a few more minutes while Cassiel stood by to make sure we didn't tear each other to shreds. Finally, I flipped Emrhys the bird and returned to my spot next to Anevae.

"I think you'd have all too much fun doing that," Emrhys snarked, but I ignored him.

Hoping Anevae could still hear me through our bond, I said, *If this is what I have to deal with for the rest of our lives, I hope there's a really good reason for you to be fated to both of these idiots. I'll do it all for you, though. If we stay—if you choose to share your life with them too—you'll have new connections to explore at some point but don't forget about me, please. I love you more than I could ever fully put into words. I'll be right here while you get some rest.*

Chapter Twenty-Two

Cassiel

As the tension in the room fizzled, I pulled the coffee table close to the couch opposite Emrhys so I could work on the prophecy. I'd already done some work on it since getting it from The Librarian, but the translated version was still extremely choppy and didn't make sense in the least. Knowing the ancient language would've been helpful, but very few around the kingdom did, as it'd been phased out several millenniums prior.

Taking a seat, I placed my stack of papers and books on the table, waiting to spread them out until Emrhys and Maeyve settled into their spots fully. The last thing I wanted was to get knee-deep into working on the prophecy and be interrupted by one—or both—of them.

Maeyve cuddled up with Anevae on the bed. Having spent the majority of my life in Baeruil, I hadn't been around many mated pairs, period. The little I did know about mates was what I'd been taught in school centuries prior. From what I remembered, bonded pairs could become inseparable to an extent, but Maeyve acted differently than I'd expected.

She seemed overly attached to her mate. When I first met them, I brushed it off as their bond being new, but I wasn't sure that was it. Her constant proximity to Anevae and unwillingness to let her out of sight seemed excessive in a way I couldn't explain. During Anevae's lessons with me, Maeyve could've easily wandered the castle, but she never did. She always sat against the wall, waiting for us to be done, as if she was afraid to let Anevae out of her sight. But, as codependent as they seemed, they were happy and could always care for each other when needed.

While the girls lay in the bed, Emrhys sat across from me, lounging back with his eyes trained on Anevae and Maeyve. The way he looked at them made me wonder if he was jealous of Maeyve. He was forced to be near them at all times. I couldn't imagine how it would feel. But I was going to be in a similar position, so I could sympathize with him.

I had been doing a lot of research on fated mates during my downtime. Not having the exposure to them left me feeling like I hardly knew anything. I wanted to understand the ins and outs of fated mates. Multiple books I'd read warned that meeting your fated mate changed your brain chemistry forever. Always having them near would make you happier. But even without completing the bond, mates never felt the same if they were separated from the one they were destined to be with; they felt like a piece of them was always missing.

My heart ached for Emrhys and me because now that we'd found her, we'd never be the same. Fate had been unkind to us both, bringing something we never thought we'd get and dangling it in front of our faces only to keep it just out of reach.

With everyone settled, I scattered my research across the tabletop and opened the tome with the prophecy. After having gotten it from The Librarian and realizing how incomplete its translation was, I'd returned to find as many books as possible about the ancient language. I wanted to try my hand at translating it on my own. But when I showed up asking The Librarian for books to help me, she warned me how few were left. I never expected that I would only find one legible, useful copy.

The oppressive weight of someone's stare fell on me as I reached to open the second tome. I tried to ignore it, but when the feeling didn't go away, I looked up at Emrhys. His gaze shifted to the papers littering the table between us. I watched him for a moment and swore I could hear the gears in his mind working overtime, trying to process something he knew very little about. At the moment, I wasn't prepared for an onslaught of questions because I still didn't know enough to explain the prophecy to anyone.

"That's a lot you've got there," Emrhys said flatly.

Sighing, I said, "It is. I've done a lot of research over the last few days. The prophecy I'm looking at was written in the ancient language, and the past attempts to translate it enclosed in this tome have been choppy at best. I'm trying to translate it myself, which is proving to be very difficult because no one knows the ancient language. You don't happen to know any of it, do you?"

"Of course I don't know the language. How old do you think I am? I'd expect you to be the one who'd know it, seeing as your kind never seem to die."

"Wow. I didn't realize how much of an asshole you can be. I was always told not to judge a book by its cover—I don't know your history, nor do you know mine—so I just wanted to make sure I wasn't overlooking anything. Sorry I asked."

Emrhys' mouth hung open as he attempted to formulate a reply. I waited a moment before returning to my research. Unbeknownst to him, during my long life, I'd met many individuals skilled in practices that had died out long before their birth. As I'd told him, I didn't want to assume he wasn't versed in the language just by judging his age; I had no ill intentions in the question I asked.

When he sharply inhaled, I glanced back at him, wanting to make sure he was okay. We may not have started on the right foot, but that didn't mean I wished harm upon him. He was fated to the same woman as me. Any harm to him would be harm to her.

With furrowed brows and cheeks a rosy pink, he said, "I, uh, I'm sorry. You're absolutely right. That was quite rude of me. Can I ask how much of this prophecy is decoded?"

It was my turn to gape at him, speechless. When I recovered, I said, "Maybe twenty-five percent, if not less. I could only find one book about the ancient language in the library of Baeruil that would even remotely help, and I'm honestly just lost with the whole process. There's so much that still doesn't make sense to me, but I'm working on it. As you can see."

"I definitely can. I'd love to offer my help, but research and puzzles aren't really my thing. Have you asked either of them?" Emrhys asked, jerking his head toward Anevae and Maeyve.

I shook my head. "I honestly don't know that I'd accept help if any of you were to offer it. I prefer to work alone and don't like it when people interrupt my processes."

"Fair enough. Do let us know if you need anything, though. This impacts us all—especially Anevae."

"I know. Thank you, Emrhys. But the most helpful thing you can do—for all of us—is to watch over her. Maeyve has done a great job so far, but she's not used to being in the castle; she seems really uneasy about being here as a whole. And she doesn't understand the threats Anevae may face being royalty, even if she's under constant supervision."

"I can hear you guys," Maeyve said from the bed, not moving.

With a nod, he relaxed back on the couch and stared longingly at Anevae again. Because he'd met her and been exposed to the potential mate bond, he'd never be the same again. If they parted ways, he'd be incomplete—lonely—for the rest of his life. But if they mated, her grandfather could find out, and all hell could break loose. The king wouldn't hesitate to kill him, no matter the impact it would have on his granddaughter or his subjects as a whole.

Maeyve, Emrhys, and I were all fucked from the moment we made contact with Anevae. Maeyve was even more so because breaking a mating bond was extremely painful and could occasionally be lethal.

Soon, we'd have to make crucial decisions that would affect our lives in Caellaias as well as the lives of those we loved. I needed to decipher the prophecy sooner rather than later because we could never see the 'later' if we made the wrong decisions somewhere in the process.

Chapter Twenty-Three

Anevae

Hushed voices woke me from the deepest sleep I'd ever experienced.

"Do you think she'll wake soon?" a man with a deep, grumbly voice asked.

"It's hard to say. It's only been a few hours," another male voice answered.

Light footsteps shuffled across the floor nearby as a woman said, "She's going to wake up soon, and everything will be fine."

"If she doesn't wake up soon, we'll have to tell the king, and he won't be pleased that we didn't tell him sooner," the second male said.

"We'll cross that bridge *if* we get there. We still have time right now," the first male voice replied with confidence.

Were they talking about me? Wait... Where was I? Who were these people? Were there more? What happened?

Unable to open my eyes, I attempted to answer one of those questions: where I was. The surface I laid on was plush and comfortable. A bed, perhaps? I'd also been covered with something soft and lightweight…like a blanket. But the exposed skin of my neck and face told me it was more for my comfort than to keep me warm.

The footsteps nearby slowed, and then the surface under me dipped. The delicious scent of vanilla and berries enveloped me—one that seemed all too familiar. Then, a breath danced across my cheek as the woman whispered, "Please wake up, my love. I know it hasn't been *that* long, but I'm tired of these two idiots already, and they won't leave until you wake."

Her voice was so sweet and seductive, like honey, that it satiated every sweet craving I'd ever had. Without thinking, I turned my head toward her, and she gasped.

"Guys, she's waking up."

Two distinct sets of footsteps hurried toward us, and the surface under me shifted twice more. The woman laid down beside me and cupped my cheek as the others settled. Her touch sent a familiar warmth through my body that I desperately wanted more of, but I couldn't get myself to move any more than I already had.

"Are you sure she's waking up?" the first man asked.

"When I came to check on her, she turned her head toward me, asshat," the woman growled.

"That doesn't mean she's waking up," the second man teased.

After a moment, the woman's voice sounded in my mind, *Anevae? Love? Please show these idiots that I'm not crazy. Okay, that's a lie. But this is one time I'm being perfectly sane.*

Her voice—her touch—was so familiar, and there was this connection between us that was so strong, almost unbreakable. But I still couldn't figure out who she was. It infuriated me.

One of the men began stroking my hair while the other grabbed my hand. Tingles shot through my body, and I realized I was connected to them in a similar manner as I was to the woman; my connections with them were just a lot weaker.

When the woman moved her hand from my face, I let out a whimper. The warmth and comfort she provided were gone immediately, and I wanted them back. Pulling my hand from one of the men's grasps, I reached for her. Latching onto her arm, I pulled her back to me.

"Don't leave. Please," I said quietly.

Pulling me into her arms, she kissed my forehead. "I'm right here. I won't go anywhere if you don't want me to."

"I-I don't remember anything."

The man with the grumbly voice sighed. "It won't last long. I allowed you to push yourself way too hard today. It won't happen again."

The other man placed his hand on my knee. "What's the last thing you remember?"

"I vaguely remember a cabin in the woods and this...beautiful woman with these mesmerizing orange eyes."

Under my head, a laugh echoed from the woman's chest. The sound brought both comfort and confusion. When I tried to push away from her—to look at her—she tightened her grip on me.

"What's so funny?" I asked, my tone harsh.

"Sorry. I'm just glad that's the last thing you remember right now. I'll let go of you in a moment, and I want you to look at me," she whispered.

When her grip loosened, I pushed myself up slowly, hoping to avoid a head rush, but it still came. I stilled and waited for the dizziness to subside. When I was finally able to open my eyes, my gaze was met by the bright orange ones I remembered so vividly. Memories began flooding me—the day I met her, our first kiss at the waterfall, the first time she touched me on my kitchen counter, when I bit her in the carriage and claimed her as mine.

Mine...my mate.

Mouth dropping, I looked around the room—my room in Caellaias. Everything came rushing back, and I gasped, whipping around to the men behind me. Emrhys and Cassiel sat there, relieved to see I was awake.

But I was livid.

I launched myself out of the bed to put space between us. Trying not to raise my voice, I asked, "What the hell happened to me in the training room? The last thing I remember is Cassiel telling me to focus on my anger. After that, things are really fuzzy."

Maeyve climbed off the bed and slowly approached me. I kept a close eye on her but allowed her too much leeway. As soon as she could reach me, she grabbed my hand, and her calming energy pulsed through me, but it didn't help.

I ripped my hand from her grasp and took several steps back. I pointed an accusatory finger at her. "Stop doing that! I know you're trying to protect me, but I need to know what happened so I can make sure it doesn't happen again. I had no clue where I was or who you all were a second ago. I don't want to feel like that again, so please, *someone* say *something* before I lose my damn mind!"

Maeyve's sadness flooded through our bond, so I turned to the two men. I couldn't deal with comforting her while I was so angry.

"Cassiel, what happened?"

Meeting my gaze, he stepped forward, but I stepped back. I didn't want anyone near me; I didn't want anyone to touch me right now.

He stopped and sighed. "You passed out while we were training."

"I remember you saying something about pushing myself too hard before I woke up. Is that true?" Cassiel nodded, so I asked, "How did you get me here?"

"I carried you from the training room. Maeyve showed me to your room because I told her I'd take you to mine if she didn't. She didn't like that idea all too much."

A small laugh bubbled in my chest, but I shoved it back down. I still wasn't in a laughing mood, but I was a little sad I missed that interaction.

The rage started to subside, confusion taking its place. "Why couldn't I remember anything?"

Cassiel rocked back on his heels and heaved out another sigh. "It's my fault. Like I said, I let you push yourself too far and didn't warn you of the possible ramifications. I just wanted to see what you were capable of. For what it's worth, I learned a lot. You're very, *very* powerful. We've only just grazed the surface of what you're capable of with your electrokinesis. I'd like to figure out how to call on any other abilities you may have soon. If you're willing to, that is. I want you to reach your full potential, Anevae."

"I appreciate that, but if it ends up like this again, it's not happening," I said sternly.

"There's a possibility it can happen anytime you use an ability for the first time or overexert yourself. You also haven't had years to grow *with* your magic like others have. It usually surfaces during childhood and grows with the user; yours has lain dormant but has grown with you still. You're learning to harness your magic when it's at its fullest potential. I will *not* let it happen again, though," said Cassiel.

Emrhys stepped up next to Cassiel, red eyes swirling. "I'm going to start attending training sessions with you guys, too. I'm your personal guard, and if anything happens to you, I need to be there."

Maeyve stalked toward me, looking at the men and snarling. When I didn't move, she closed the distance between us and wrapped me in her arms.

Relaxing into her, I looked at Cassiel. "When it comes to my magic, I'm doing things on my own terms from now on." Then, I shifted my gaze to Emrhys. "And I don't need you to come to my lessons."

"I t—" Cassiel started, but Emrhys interrupted.

"You know what? Let's discuss this later. It's almost time for dinner, and your grandfather doesn't know anything about what occurred during your lessons, so he'll be expecting you. Cass and I can wait in the hallway while you change for dinner."

Chapter Twenty-Four

Emrhys

After Cassiel rounded up his things, we stepped into the hall as I'd promised. A heavy tension clouded the space between us, likely due to the way I'd acted during Anevae's slumber. She'd been in his presence when she became incapacitated, which put me on edge. If anything had happened to her, it would have been my ass on the line—not his.

When the door was shut behind us, Cassiel said, "You don't need to attend our training sessions. I am more than capable of taking care of her while she's under my watch. Not to mention, with you there, she'll be even more distracted than when it's just Maeyve and I."

I smirked. "Ah, but you see, I'm her personal guard. I think it would make perfect sense for me to be there. You know...to keep her *safe*. Because if *anything* happens to her, I will be the first person they come to with questions."

He crossed his arms and frowned. "You don't trust me, do you?"

"No. Especially after the shit you pulled today. That was so stupid! She could've gotten hurt. Before you let her harness her magic, did you even explain anything? Or did you just let her go at it?"

His jaw ticked as he shook his head. "I made sure she had a good grasp on things, then instructed her to hit the targets I'd laid out. I had th—"

"No wonder she overdid it! You can't just start by seeing what someone is capable of. You have to start off slow. I don't even have magic, and I know that. Have you ever been an instructor before?" When he shook his head again, I huffed out a breath. "This is why I need to be there. Who actually employed you? Because I don't feel like this is something the king would've allowed had he known."

"We all have to start somewhere. You didn't start as a royal guard, did you? You worked your way up the ranks. This is my starting point. I know I fucked up, okay? My judgment is slightly distorted, especially because this woman could be my *mate.* An angel has never had one before."

I ground my teeth together as I mulled everything over. "Fine. But I will be attending her lessons starting tomorrow, whether you like it or not. I don't want you near her alone anymore. I won't let you put her in danger again. And I haven't forgotten about the gods damned prophecy you won't tell us about. The second you know more, you need to tell us."

"I told you, I had things under control when she harnessed her magic. It takes time, and like I told her, she didn't have a chance to grow with her magic like others have. For her sake, just chill out. I am working on the prophecy, but it's going to take me a while to figure it out. There are still so many unknowns. But if it means what I think it does, she's not going to be able to return to the human realm."

My lips parted, and my stomach sank. She could be stuck in Caellaias after all. As much as it would kill me for her to leave, I didn't want her to suffer. She loved her home in the human realm, where she felt comfortable and at peace. Every piece of Caellaias she unearthed made her want to return to the human realm and the life she knew.

But even without the prophecy, it was clear that she was meant for so much more than that.

When I met Cassiel's gaze again, he nodded. "That's what I thought. Anyway, I'm not invited to dinner, so I'll take my leave. Have a good evening." Then, he snapped his fingers, and he was gone.

Huffing, I hustled to my room to get ready for dinner. When I sensed something was off with Anevae, I threw on whatever clothes I could find to check on her. While they weren't indecent, the king would not be pleased if I didn't show up dressed appropriately; he expected perfection from everyone in the castle.

The trek to gather my clothing gave me time to mull over the prophecy. I'd never paid much attention to them. Most of the kingdom didn't really believe in prophecies, but the angels took them very seriously. I wasn't sure how much it could really affect her life, but if it was right about her having multiple mates, then I wanted to know what else it said.

Thanks to my speed, I was able to retrieve my things and get back to Anevae's door in just a few minutes. Upon returning, I took note that Aeros wasn't at his post. But it wasn't my business, so I tried to brush it aside. Eirian wasn't mine to protect.

A minute later, Anevae's door swung open. She strode out wearing a beautiful pale purple gown with gold accents. By the gods, she was beautiful—the most beautiful woman I'd ever laid eyes upon—and I wanted her so much it hurt. My heart fluttered when she met my gaze, but she looked away quickly.

Maeyve followed closely behind her out the door in an emerald green gown that hugged all her curves in just the right places. When she reached for Anevae, jealousy sunk its claws into me; her presence would always be a bitter reminder of what I couldn't have.

When I joined the ranks, I had accepted the fact that I would never have time to find my fated mate; I'd dedicated my life to my work. But now that I'd found her and wasn't allowed to have her, things were a million times worse. It was a torment I'd never be allowed to escape.

The door clicked shut behind Maeyve, and she cleared her throat, demanding my attention. After taking a shallow breath, I gave them a weak smile and escorted them to the dining hall, acting as if there wasn't a war raging inside of me.

Chapter Twenty-Five

Anevae

Dinner went by swiftly that night. When we were done, my grandfather dismissed us, and Emrhys escorted Maeyve and me back to our suite.

As soon as we reached the stairs, Maeyve was in my head. *I need you more than I can explain right now.*

Biting my lip piercing, I responded, *You always need me—in more ways than one.*

Behind me, Maeyve chuckled. *If anything, you're the one who always needs me. You jump at me every chance you get. I'm lucky I get any sleep around you!*

Excuse me? It's not like you're any better. And you're a succubus! How do I know you aren't using your abilities on me?

Don't put this back on me. You know exactly what it feels like when I use my abilities. Have you felt that fire, sweetheart?

My cheeks reddened. Even though she didn't seem hurt by my teasing, I felt bad even jokingly accusing her of it. Though remembering how it felt had my clit throbbing with need. Part of me wanted her to do it—to teach me a lesson and show me what it was like again and again.

The walk up the stairs seemed to last forever because I knew what was in store for me when I got to my room. But it was almost like Emrhys could sense that I was antsy to get there, and he slowed as we neared the top of the staircase.

Taking one more step, he let out a loud sigh. "Can you guys stop thinking about whatever it is that you're thinking about for like five minutes? Your arousal is overwhelming. Once you get inside your room, you can do whatever you want to each other. I just c—"

"Awww. Are you jealous that you can't join us, Em?" Maeyve teased.

Emrhys clenched his hands, and he continued toward my room. I followed him, but my thoughts got the best of me, imagining how it would feel to have them both touching me. My pussy throbbed, begging me to invite him into my bed, and I fought it. I tried to remind myself of what he'd done to make me hate him. My body didn't care; it desperately wanted him.

I rolled my lip between my teeth in an attempt to keep the thoughts at bay—at least until we got to my room—but they kept coming. My only hope was that they weren't projecting into Maeyve's mind through our bond. I was so stuck in my thoughts I hadn't realized Emrhys had stopped in the middle of the hall and ran right into him.

Whirling around, he grabbed me before I could fall and held me by the shoulders. I was so close he only needed to speak in a whisper for me to hear him. "Did the thought of me joining you arouse you more?"

It took me a moment, but I looked up at him through my lashes and nodded. I hated to admit it, but I wanted him. I didn't know if I could deny it anymore.

"Oh, princess, all you have to do is ask. I'll gladly join you if you want me to," he said in a deep, sultry voice as he ran his hand up my shoulder to my cheek, his touch sending his warmth throughout my body.

My cheeks flushed as I considered Emrhys's offer, but Maeyve's irritation flared through our bond. I wasn't sure she had heard him, and I was even less sure she'd be okay with him joining us. I'd never been part of a threesome, nor had I ever practiced polyamory in the past, but it'd always intrigued me.

I was conflicted about what to do until Maeyve stepped in closer and placed her hands on my hips. *As much as I want to keep you all to myself, he's fated to you, too. If what you're feeling for him is anything like what I felt for you in the beginning, I can understand. He hasn't done right by you in the past, but he's changed his tune since he found out you were supposed to be his. If you want him to join us, just say the word. If you want time with just him to explore each other, that's okay, too.*

My fear eased, but I forced myself to consider everything that had happened between Emrhys and me. Since he'd found out we were fated, he'd been extremely protective of me and had proven that he really cared about me. I didn't think I could ignore my feelings for him forever. Just how he acted told me he was already struggling to keep himself together. He wanted me...*needed* me. If he didn't have me soon, he would break, and I wasn't far behind him.

"I want you both in my bed tonight. I can't deny how I feel about you anymore, Emrhys. I need you to be buried so deep inside of me I forget what's happening outside of my bedroom walls."

Maeyve's tension eased through the bond. Gently, she planted a kiss on my neck. *As you wish, my love.*

When the words registered to Emrhys, a wicked smile spread across his face. Part of me regretted inviting him into my bed because this would change so many things for us. He'd no longer just be my guard and attempted kidnapper. Things would be different and could potentially become more at some point.

Catching me off guard, he lifted me into his arms. On instinct, I clutched his shoulders and wrapped my legs around his middle, where

I was met with his erection pressing against my clit. When he started moving, my body rocked up and down, putting delicious friction on the sensitive area. To keep myself from moaning, I placed kisses along his jaw.

Maeyve moved around us to open the door and, through the bond, said, *I didn't know this would turn me on so much. Fuck. I almost just want to sit back and watch him fuck you into oblivion.*

A small moan escaped my lips as Emrhys crossed the threshold into my room. "You have too many fucking clothes on," he grumbled as he threw me down on the bed. "I've wanted to do this since the first time I saw you in your cabin. You were so beautiful and peaceful. I didn't want to kidnap you against your will—to ruin your peace—but I couldn't defy your grandfather without risking my position. Now that you're so close all the time, I struggle not to break every damn rule, risk my life, and claim you every time you're within arms reach."

My heart stuttered at his words. I'd spent the last few weeks hating him for everything he'd done to me and fighting the feelings I'd had for him. During that time, he did as he was told, and he'd been suffering. He wanted me, even though I'd treated him awfully. He'd tried to protect me from the things I knew little about.

I captured Emrhys' lips with mine before he moved to climb off the bed. Then, I said, "One of you needs to help me out of this dress before I lose my nerve."

Maeyve huffed out a small laugh as she helped me to my feet. "I have a sneaking suspicion that you wouldn't lose your nerve. You want him more than you realize. Your body is dying to connect with his. Now, be a good girl and turn around so I can unlace this corset."

I did as she asked, turning to face Emrhys. The red of his irises intensified as he took a step closer to me. My heart rate sped up when Maeyve pulled the first string loose on my corset. After she pulled a couple more, Emrhys flicked the straps off my shoulders, and the fabric fell to the floor, exposing me completely save for my panties, which left little to the imagination.

Emrhys' gaze traveled down my body, and he groaned. "You're so fucking perfect. Fuck. It's going to be so hard not to mate with you the moment I sink my cock into that soaking wet cunt."

Biting my lip piercing, I closed the distance between us and placed my hands on his chest. "Now you're the one with too many clothes on."

Smirking down at me, he rested his hands on my bare hips. Tingles spread throughout my body, and I gripped his shirt tightly as another moan slipped past my lips.

He grazed his hands down my hips, and they stopped at the curve of my ass, lifting me again with ease. "Those sounds coming from your lips are a drug, and I don't think I can ever get enough."

I wrapped myself around him and whispered, "Why don't you get these clothes off and see what other sounds you can get me to make? Or are you too scared?"

Walking us to the bed, he laid me down. "I'm not scared of anything as long as I have you. Fuck your grandfather. From this night forward, you are mine, and he cannot change that. I don't care what he threatens me with. I never thought I'd find the one fated to me, and I will not let him take you from me—ever. You are *mine*." When the last words left his lips, he pushed himself off the bed. It felt like a piece of me left with him.

Maeyve took his place and ripped my panties off in one swift motion.

"You know how hard it was for me to get those! Don't be ruining the few pairs I have left," I whined.

Maeyve snickered and planted a kiss on my thigh. "I like it better when you don't have them anyway."

The sensations they caused in my body were the same but completely different. I ached to know how it would feel when they both touched me at the same time. She planted a kiss on the other thigh, then backed up, revealing Emrhys, who was completely undressed. I trailed my eyes down his body, stopping on his thick cock at full attention.

The sight of him had me soaking wet within an instant.

Slowly, he approached the edge of the bed. "I feel like I've waited an eternity for this moment."

Biting my lip, I lifted myself onto my elbows. When he continued to stand there for a moment, I smirked. "Then get up here and fuck me like I know you want to."

After a breathy laugh, he said, "That mouth will get you into trouble one day. Now, be a good girl and spread those legs for me."

"Maybe you should make me."

A Cheshire grin crept across his face as he stalked toward the bed. As the mattress shifted under his weight, my heart skipped a beat. I loved to give Emrhys attitude outside of the bedroom, but the way he reacted when I was a brat and talked back to him made me melt. I didn't care about the consequences; I wanted him to dominate me. Crawling up the bed, he placed kisses on my leg. The sensation of his soft lips and bristly beard against my leg initially caused me to jump, but when he placed his hand on the outside of my thigh, I relaxed. He continued to trail kisses up my leg until he reached the apex of my thighs.

"Spread those legs, princess. I want to taste you."

Giving him a look of defiance, I shook my head and pressed my thighs closer together.

"You're testing my patience. I'll gladly flip you over and spank you so hard you won't be able to sit for days."

Still, I refused, but his threat had me rubbing my thighs together in anticipation.

"I'm only going to say it one more time. Spread. Those. Legs."

His commanding voice broke my resolve, and I laid back, allowing my legs to fall open.

"That's a good girl," he said before he began kissing up my thigh. When he reached the apex of my thighs again, he looked back up at me. "You smell delectable. I can't wait to taste you. Are you ready, princess?"

"Yes," I panted.

"Mmm. You're so wet for me," he said, then licked his lips.

When he didn't do anything, I wiggled my hips impatiently. I needed some kind of stimulation. Just laying there with his mouth so close was torture.

"Patience."

"Emrhys, please," I whimpered. He tsked, which only made me more irritated. "Please do something, or I'll have Maeyve take over for you."

"So impatient. That won't get you far. Not to mention, Maeyve won't save you from me."

Grabbing the sheets beside me, I let out a frustrated groan. When I tried to sit up, Emrhys' hand was on my belly, pushing me back down. Looking down at him, he was glaring at me.

"Lay. Back. I'm not done with you," he growled.

"Then fucking do something besides teasing me," I demanded.

Leaning in, he kept eye contact with me as he licked up my wet slit. Throwing my head back, I let out a soft moan.

"You taste even better than you smell," he said, humming his delight before diving in for more.

After a moment, I started rocking my hips into his mouth. His fangs grazed my clit once, twice, and then I was exploding against his tongue. My release hit me so hard that an almost primal sound erupted from my throat. Emrhys continued his pursuit, sucking my clit into his mouth, and I began shaking to my core. Reaching down, I grabbed a handful of his hair, trying to pull him away, but it was pointless. He continued sucking and licking my clit until another orgasm crested. My grip on his hair tightened as I began riding his face, chasing my climax. When my orgasm pushed me over the edge, his name was on my lips.

Panting, I relaxed my grip on Emrhys' hair and sank into the bed. I was still a shaking mess, but when he released my clit, his teeth lightly grazed it, and I shivered. After two orgasms, I was overly sensitive. I wasn't sure I could handle another.

Emrhys raised himself onto his knees and licked every last bit of my arousal from his lips. "If your blood tastes half as good as your pussy, I'm not going to be able to keep my hands off you."

"Is that a promise? So far, you're all bark and no bite, so I don't know if I believe you."

"That's a fact," he said as he lowered himself to place kisses up my body. When he reached my breasts, he licked circles around each nipple. I arched my back into him, enjoying the heat of his breath against my skin. He skimmed his fingertips over my side, coming up to caress the breast he licked.

After one last stroke of his tongue, he looked up at me. "Whatever these things are through your nipples, I like them."

A smile crept across my face. "They're called barbells, but the thing in general is a piercing."

"I've never seen one like this. You have so many of these...piercings. But they all suit you so well. These are my favorite, though."

I let out a small laugh as he scooted up and nestled himself between my legs, teasing the tip of his cock at my entrance. I inhaled sharply and gripped the sheets beside me. It'd been a while since I'd had sex with a man, and I was still sensitive from the two orgasms I'd had moments before.

"Relax," he said softly.

After a deep breath, I released the sheets, reaching up to grip his shoulders instead. His heated gaze bore into me, silently asking if I was ready. I rocked my hips in response, and he smiled.

"You might just be the death of me, princess."

Then, he swooped down, and his lips collided with mine in a messy, desperate kiss. Parting my lips, I slipped my tongue into his mouth and dug my nails into his shoulders. I couldn't take it anymore; I needed him inside me.

Slipping my tongue out of his mouth, I bit down on his lip. When I released it, I whispered, "Stop teasing me and fuck me already."

Without warning, he sheathed himself inside of me, and I gripped his shoulders even tighter as I screamed. With my mouth open, he bit down on my lip lightly. He tugged on it with his teeth, then released it. As he did, he pulled almost all the way out of me before slamming back in. But then he stopped, staring down at me with concern in his questioning gaze.

I panted, "Keep going."

That was all the permission he needed before his lips crashed back against mine, and he started pounding into me.

I'd almost forgotten Maeyve was there until she climbed on the bed beside me, completely naked. *Is he hurting you?*

No. Fuck, no, he's not at all, I said in return as he continued pounding into me.

He sat up on his knees and spread my legs wide. The new angle had him driving deeper into me and hitting just the right spot up high. Trying not to scream too loud, I reached up to cover my mouth, but Maeyve caught my hands and pinned them above my head.

"Let them all hear the sounds you make for us while we please you. Don't worry about anyone outside this room. Focus on how it feels to have Emrhys pound into you while you're pinned down." When I closed my eyes and did as she instructed, she whispered, "That's our good little slut. Do you like it when we both touch you?"

I'd never thought I was into dirty talk, but she knew all the right things to say. I nodded with desperate enthusiasm. "Yes."

While she held my hands, she glanced up at Emrhys with a smirk. "Should we show her what she gets when she's a very good girl?"

Chapter Twenty-Six

Emrhys

"**M**aybe that'll teach her to stop being such a brat," I said as I slowed my pace.

Anevae bucked her hips, trying to ride me from where she lay, and roared out in frustration when I pulled out of her. Maeyve and I laughed at her attempts.

When she began flailing, I grabbed her hips and lined myself up again. "So much for showing you what you get when you're a good girl." As the last word left my lips, I slammed into her.

The impact had her crying out and arching her back, but I stopped all movement, leaving myself buried to the hilt inside her. If she were going to be a brat, she would be treated like one. My bruising grip on her hips kept her from moving as I decided what to do next.

"Are you going to be a good girl, Anevae?" I asked.

Breathing heavily, she looked at me with pursed lips and furrowed brows. "Fuck you."

"Ah, but you already are," I said, pulling out and slamming back into her. "I'm only asking one more time...Are. You. Going. To. Be. A. Good. Girl?"

Her nostrils flared as she growled, "No. I don't think I will."

Maeyve tsked, sitting back on her haunches. "We could've had so much more fun if you'd behaved."

Releasing Anevae's hips, I came down on top of her, pinning her down with my body. "I think you've forgotten who you're talking to—what I'm capable of."

"I haven't forgotten shit. I rather like mouthing off to you...getting under your skin," Anevae said, a smile playing on her lips.

Hovering my mouth over hers, I said, "I think you're going to regret saying that." After a quick kiss, I sat up.

"I highly doubt it. This has been so much fun. Roll those hips into me, baby. Fuck my pretty little cunt like you've dreamt of. It's yours for the taking now."

My cock jerked inside of her, urging me to continue what I'd started. Slowly, I pumped in and out of her a couple of times, enjoying just how perfectly we fit together. Continuing short, languid strokes, I bent over and sucked one of her nipples in my mouth. Rolling my tongue around the stiff peak, I gently flicked the piercing a few times.

When Anevae wrapped her legs around my waist, I struck, biting her breast. Her back bowed off the bed, and her pussy tightened around my cock as she let out a guttural cry. Maeyve quickly muffled the cry with a kiss, and I retracted my teeth as her orgasm crested. I took a long pull of her blood and slammed into her, walls still fluttering around me.

As her sweet blood coated my tongue and made its way down my throat, an inhuman sound rumbled in my chest. Then, a shock rippled through my body, and I stilled. Had her magic surface? Anevae lay as still as possible through her panting, and Maeyve continued to hover over her, brows furrowed in confusion. Once some of the fear eased, I flicked my tongue over one of my fangs and gathered a drop of my blood to close the puncture marks on Anevae's breast. When the wounds were taken care of, I licked up what blood I could.

Sitting up, I looked into Anevae's eyes and was shocked to see the blue of her irises surrounded by red. Before I could address it, though, I found myself on my back, straddled by her. Had she flipped us?

"What the hell just happened?" she asked, staring daggers at me.

I threw up my hands in defense. "I-I'm not sure. I've never felt anything like that when I've bitten someone. I thought it was your magic or something." Trailing my eyes down to inspect her breast, I saw the bite mark and knew immediately what had happened. Dropping my hands, I closed my eyes and whispered, "Fuck."

Anevae's hands came down on my chest hard. "What the fuck is that supposed to mean? What did you do?"

Taking a deep breath, I opened my eyes to meet her gaze. "It appears that I've initiated a mate bond with you."

Dropping her head, she murmured, "Fuck."

Maeyve appeared above me and lifted Anevae's chin. "He's already started the bond. If you don't complete it now, it's going to get more and more difficult for you to fight off. As much as I hate to say it, maybe it was meant to happen this way."

Anevae ripped her chin away from her mate. "Don't use my words against me." Then, she looked back down at me. "How do I complete the bond with you? I'm not a vampire, so I can't just bite you like you did with me...can I?"

A lopsided smirk crept across my face as I ran my fingertips up and down her thighs. "You are part shifter, though. Judging by the marks on both your necks, your bond with Maeyve was sealed by a bite."

My dick, somehow still hard through the tension, twitched inside of her, and her nails dug into my chest. Even though she was undoubtedly sensitive, her eyes locked onto mine, hooded with lust again.

Sliding my hands up to her hips, I gripped them tightly, and my smile widened. I thrust up into her hard and said, "You've had three orgasms now, and I've had none. Ride me like your life depends on it, then sink your teeth into my skin, marking me so the kingdom knows I'm yours."

Her heart rate increased as she rolled her bottom lip into her mouth again. That single action made me want to flip her back over and pin her below me. While she considered my request, she lifted herself until I was barely inside her, then slammed back down on me. My mouth dropped open as I let out a ragged breath. This woman would be the death of me. Whether it was going to be a good or a bad death was still up in the air, but I didn't care anymore. She was going to be *mine*.

"I don't want to fight this anymore. I *need* you. But, I swear, if you end up dead or separated from me—all because *you* bit me—I will show no mercy to those who have wronged us," she said, rolling her hips.

"I won't let that happen, princess. They'll have to pry you from my cold, dead hands. I will destroy the whole kingdom if that means I never have to leave your side."

Her mouth came crashing down on mine, and I wrapped my arms tighter around her, thrusting into her like it would be the last time I'd ever have her in my arms. I knew it wouldn't be, but I held onto her as tight as I could, relishing the feel of her skin against mine.

When our lips broke contact, she kissed along my jaw and then down my neck. I loosened my grip, knowing what was about to happen. I was ready for it—to be bound to the one person I was convinced I'd never find...damn the consequences.

After what felt like an eternity, she placed one last kiss on my shoulder. My body shook with anticipation. She nibbled at my skin, her canines grazing it, and I saw stars. Then she bit me; the sharp points of her teeth pierced my skin, and pain mixed with pleasure. My nails dug into her skin, drawing blood, as an orgasm more intense than I'd ever had ripped through me. When she withdrew her teeth, my blood trickled into her mouth, and a small moan resounded from her throat.

Once my grip on her loosened, she slid her tongue over the bite—cleaning up the blood and healing the wound at the same time—before kissing me and resting her forehead against mine. We lay there for several moments, my fingertips drawing lazy circles across her bare back. I didn't want to let her go. When she moved off me, we'd have to figure out how we would navigate our relationship.

Are you okay? Anevae's voice said, but it was most certainly not aloud.

My fingers stilled. "Did you—"

Yes. That's a 'perk of being mated,' as Maeyve told me when she did it the first time. We can speak telepathically, and I can project things into your mind. Moments later, an image of Anevae and Maeyve naked and kissing popped into my head.

As unsettling as that is, it'll be really useful in the future. But that image is already making me hard again. You ready for another round, princess? I said as I flipped us over and kissed her nose.

Anevae giggled and pushed on my shoulders. "I think that's enough for now."

"You're no fun."

"You share that belief with Maeyve, apparently. But I need a bath and some time with my *first* mate. You'll see me tomorrow, I promise. Plus, we can't afford to raise any suspicions. Our luck, Aeros is in the hall right now listening to everything anyway."

Rocking back onto my haunches, my hand flew to my chest. "Am I not important, too?"

She rolled her eyes and sat up. "Out of everything I just said, *that* is what you held onto? You're not worried at all about Aeros running back to the king? We just had very loud, very intense sex. You need to go, and Maeyve needs some time with me."

"Fine, but I get to join next time. Watching you eat her out the other night was hot."

With a scoff, Anevae and Maeyve climbed out of bed and into the bath while I dressed. Before leaving the room, I strolled over to where Anevae sat in the tub and pulled her chin up, gently kissing her lips. She was mine now. No one could take her from me.

I closed the door lightly as I left, only to find Aeros standing across the hall. He had a smug look on his face, telling me he'd heard enough of what happened in the bedroom.

"Finally got a piece of it, huh?" he teased.

"What happened in there is none of your business."

"Aww. Em, come on. I've been rooting for you. Better not let the king find out, though. We know how much that'll upset him."

"Don't fucking call me that. We are not friends, and we never will be. And, you know what? I don't give a fuck what the king will think. She's—" I cut myself off before the words slipped through my lips. I couldn't let him know that she was my fated mate—that she was *mine* now. Even though I brushed off Anevae's concern, I was still afraid he would tell the king what he thought happened in Anevae's room.

"She's what?" he asked, eyes full of curiosity.

"She's been traumatized enough by the asshole in the short amount of time she's known him."

"Oooh. Someone has opinions about the king. I always thought you were the one who had his back—his trusty little servant who does everything he commands. Isn't that what got you this job in the first place?"

"I don't have to explain anything to you. Fuck off."

Letting out a breathy laugh, he leaned back against the wall. "Glad to see that getting a little pussy doesn't change you."

I didn't give him the satisfaction of a response before I stomped down the hall to my room. I needed to wash up and get back outside Anevae's door. Unfortunately, I'd have to start getting up earlier to attend training with her. Cassiel had broken my trust, and while Maeyve had done a great job protecting her, I'd staked my claim on her, and I didn't want to put her care in anyone else's hands ever again.

I made the water as hot as I could before stepping into the shower. It scalded my skin at first—especially my brand new, still sore mating mark—but the heat and pain served to distract me from the thoughts running through my mind. If the king found out what happened in that bedroom, he could excuse me from my station. If he discovered I'd mated with his granddaughter, he would sentence me to death. That frightened me beyond belief, especially with what Anevae said before she bit me. I wasn't sure how we were going to make things work, but we'd have to find a way. We were mated, and I wouldn't let someone take away the one thing I'd always craved and never thought I'd have.

I finished my shower and dressed. Then, I hurried back down the hall to watch over the woman who'd captured my heart.

Chapter Twenty-Seven

Cassiel

The next morning, Maarya wasn't the one to escort Anevae and Maeyve to the training room. Despite my assurances of Anevae's safety to Emrhys, he decided to accompany them. He seemed different in some way, but I couldn't put my finger on what it was. He was much happier than when I'd left him outside Anevae's room the day before. She looked a lot happier, too. There was a pep in her step I hadn't seen before, and she was hanging out awfully close to the vampire.

When Anevae stopped before me, I took her hand and brought it to my lips for a soft kiss. "Good morning, Anevae."

Emrhys and Maeyve stiffened, their reactions sending a wave of satisfaction through me. I wasn't sure what Emrhys was getting at, but if he wanted to play games, I'd show him just how dirty I could play.

Anevae raised an eyebrow as she slid her hand from mine. "Good morning, Cassiel. What are the plans for today? Do I have to go back to my history lessons after yesterday's fiasco?"

A smile crept across my face as I shifted to clasp my hands behind my back. "No, I won't make you return to the history lessons for now. You already know a good chunk about the land. And I know how anxious you are to understand your magic."

She breathed a sigh of relief, but behind her, Emrhys stiffened. I would not let his fears become a reality. I meant it when I told him I would be closely monitoring her. I had no intention of pushing her that hard again. Now that she knew better, I doubted Anevae would let it happen either.

I continued, "I've set up more targets for you to work with, but we're going to be moving much slower. I do *not* want another incident like yesterday. It was partially my fault, but if you're not feeling well during this—even the slightest bit—I need you to tell me. Do not push yourself any further than you need to." Anevae nodded, and I said, "Perfect. We can begin when you're ready."

As she approached the targets, I joined Emrhys and Maeve. "Neither of you need to be here. You're just going to be distractions for her."

"We'd both feel a lot more comfortable being here with her. Right, Em?" Maeyve said, looking to Emrhys for backup.

"Yes. I think the more eyes on her, the better."

I crossed my arms and gave them a distrusting look. "Did something happen last night that you'd like to share with the class? Something is...different between you three."

"What happened last night is none of your concern," Emrhys snapped.

"It's absolutely my concern if we're all to be mated to her one day. She's just as much mine as she is yours. Now, get off your high fucking horse. I just want what's best for her."

He narrowed his eyes and took a step toward me. "*I* am here to make sure you don't put her in harm's way. *Again*. And, as we deduced yesterday, I don't fucking trust you, so why would I tell you if something happened between us last night?"

I gave him a devilish grin. "I'm more capable of protecting her than you think."

"That doesn't change the fact that you put her in danger yesterday. We're not leaving," he hissed.

"I could've easily diffused the situation if it was necessary, and Maeyve was here with her calming abilities at the ready. It's not like she went on a killing spree. She was more in control than you think," I said, nostrils flaring before I walked away.

This wouldn't be the end of our conversation by a long shot. He'd continue challenging me until he knew what I hoped to prepare her for.

I placed my hand on Anevae's lower back. "Are you ready to get started, darling?"

She jumped at the touch but then smiled up at me. Peering around me, she asked, "Why are Maeyve and Emrhys all the way over in the corner? They were adamant about coming with me. I was sure they'd also want to be part of my training."

"I asked them to leave us be for a while. They won't be able to help you with this first little bit I teach you. They don't possess this type of magic, nor do they understand how it works. Once you've mastered attacking the inanimate targets, I'll gladly invite them to join us so you can use them as targets, too."

Anevae let out a breathy laugh. "Haha. Very funny. I will not be using any of you three as targets anytime in the near future. If you guys start to piss me off, I may revisit the idea," she said with a smirk.

A light chuckle left my lips. "Sounds good. Let's start over here," I said as I led her to the wall of mirrors where I'd placed two cushions on the floor. "I'm sure you're not going to like this piece, but it's probably the most important skill when learning to *control* your magic."

"Okay?" she said, eyeing the cushions with suspicion.

"This floor isn't comfortable, so the cushions are to help with that. The mirrors are so you can see what happens when you wield your magic, but that will be a little later. Please, have a seat."

After settling on the cushion, she met my eyes in the mirror. "What exactly are we doing?"

"We're going to meditate—"

Not even letting me finish, she let out a groan. "Anything but this, please? I've tried to meditate in the past, but I can't ever turn my brain off."

"No one ever said you had to turn your brain off. Meditation can be used to assess what's happening inside yourself—including your mind. This is how most magic users discover the best way to call forth their magic and keep it under control. Just...give me a chance to guide you through one session. If it doesn't work, we'll find another way. Deal?"

"Fine. Let's do it."

"Thank you," I said as I sat on my own cushion. When we were both situated, I met her gaze in the mirror again. "First, I want you to close your eyes and focus on your breathing." Once I was sure she was following my instructions, I closed my eyes and did the same.

"Okay. Now what?"

"Patience, darling. Focus on your breathing for another minute." After a minute of no further protests, I said, "Now, with each breath, I want you to unclench your jaw and remove your tongue from the roof of your mouth. Then, focus on relaxing your shoulders. When they're relaxed, move on to another part of your body until there aren't any tight muscles anywhere."

I opened my eyes and watched her walk through each piece of her body, the tension slowly easing from her face as each area was relaxed. Several minutes later, she looked to be at peace both inside and out.

"Perfect. How—"

"Hold on, please. I need another moment of quiet."

A smile crept across my lips. Respecting her wishes, I waited for her to let me know when she was ready, but after a few minutes, she opened her eyes and turned to me.

"I wa—" I began again, but then her eyes caught my attention, and I froze. Her irises, normally a deeper blue, had become the color of an orletaylaer—exactly the same color as mine—with tiny flecks of red throughout, engulfed in a ring of yellow. "Your abilities have all surfaced, haven't they?" I asked in a hushed tone.

"I-I think so. When everything relaxed, this sudden warmth started in my fingertips and toes. That's about when you started talking, and I knew if I stopped focusing on it, I wouldn't be able to get it back. When the warmth reached my chest, it was like I was thrown into a pool filled with hot water as it engulfed my entire body. Now, it's like I feel the undercurrent of electricity from my magic beneath my skin, and it doesn't go away. Other things feel different, too, but I don't completely understand them right now."

"Do me a favor. Trying to conjure up a *small* electricity ball." Her brows knitted together, so I placed my hand on hers and said, "You're not going to hurt anyone. I promise I'd never let that happen. And you're not going to push it too far, either. I'm right here, and the other two are across the room watching us like hawks."

Chapter Twenty-Eight

Anevae

Maeyve and Emrhys kept their distance during the entire training, as Cassiel had asked, surprising the hell out of me. Neither of them had even reached out through our bonds when my abilities surfaced. Cassiel helped me work with my electrokinesis for a while, but it proved quite tricky when I tried to call my glamour magic to the surface. Very little was known about it since it was such a unique type of magic specific to the royals, and I instantly wished my mom was around to help me; she would've known how to help me.

A few hours later, my body was run down and exhausted, so we stopped. I looked across the room to where my mates sat and chuckled. They were sitting in similar positions: arms crossed over their chests and legs extended with the left foot crossed over the right. The night prior had unlocked some sort of understanding between the two. I wasn't just mated to Maeyve anymore, and they'd be sharing me for the rest of our lives—unless one of our bonds was broken.

Cassiel approached. "Would you like some help up? You did very well today."

Smiling, I took his hand, comforted by his skin against mine and the way his bond called to me. "Thank you. It helps that you're a good teacher."

He pulled me to my feet and whispered his thanks. Once I was on my feet, he skimmed his hand up my arm to my cheek, leaving a trail of goosebumps in its wake.

Seemingly out of nowhere, Emrhys appeared beside me, nostrils flared and eyes a vivid, swirling red. "Hands off her."

Cassiel's gaze shifted from his usual teal to a blinding white. When he spoke, his voice was different—deeper and full of power. "You already know damn well that I will not *ever* let harm come to her. Anevae is capable of making her own decisions about who she wants around her. You—"

Shoving Cassiel away, I stepped between him and Emrhys. "That is *enough!* I am no one's property. I will not have you fighting over me as if this is a game of fucking tug-o-war." Both men frowned. But when my gaze turned more severe, Cassiel's eyes returned to normal, and Emrhys relaxed. "Thank you. If you two keep acting like this, only one of you will be allowed with me at any given time. I can't imagine what either of you will be like if I'm mated to you both."

Emrhys clenched his jaw tightly as he stared Cassiel down. After several tense seconds, Cassiel averted his gaze back to me and said, "I think we should take this conversation elsewhere. I have some things I need to discuss with you all anyway."

"No one's in here but us, so why not here?" I asked.

Emrhys took a deep breath. "Because your grandfather has eyes and ears all over this place. The servants do a great job staying hidden, but they listen to everything we say and watch everything we do. Then, they report back to the king's advisor with their findings."

"Welp. Just another reason for me to despise him. What does my sister see in him that I don't?"

Emrhys laughed. "He treats her differently because she minds her manners and listens to him. You're more of a wild and free spirit like your mom. Your disobedience pushes every one of his buttons and reminds him that he's not in control with you."

Cassiel smiled and tilted my chin up to look at him. "I'll meet you three in your room in about an hour. I need to gather some things."

"Please be careful," I whispered.

"You act like I'm going on some sort of high-profile mission or something. I'll see you in a little bit," he said with a playful tone. Before releasing my chin, he lightly kissed my lips and forehead. Then, he was gone.

I scowled at my remaining mates, nostrils flared, and hissed, "You two need to get your panties out of a twist. I am yours as much as you are mine. Let's fucking go. The quicker I learn what's going on, the better."

Without another word, I stomped out of the training room and back up the stairs to my room. When we reached the top of the landing, Emrhys darted in front of me to check out my suite. Maeyve and I were about halfway down the hall when he reappeared outside my door. As we approached, he stepped aside to let us in and closed the door behind us.

Chapter Twenty-Nine

Emrhys

When I closed the door behind Anevae and Maeyve, my mind was going a million miles a minute, and I couldn't get it to calm down. I was anxious to know if Cassiel had found out more about the prophecy and if it was, in fact, linked to Anevae.

As I stood there, Anevae reappeared, looking at me with an expecting gaze.

"What can I do for you, princess?" I asked quietly.

"Are you just going to stand out in the hallway and act like you aren't already invited inside? Like you aren't dying to be near me at all times? Because, even though I'm angry with you, I don't want you out of my sight."

A smirk appeared on my face. "Do we get to have angry sex? Because angry sex is *hot.*"

Her arousal spiked, but she rolled her eyes. "You're impossible. Cassiel will be here soon, so come on."

"You didn't say no…Ooh. A four-way does sound like a lot of fun. I'm not ki—"

"Emrhys! Seriously? Just get in the damn room before I change my mind."

Letting out a small laugh, I strode in and closed the door behind me. Anevae's arousal hit me hard the moment I crossed the threshold of her room, and I couldn't stop my growing erection. They hadn't lied when they said newly mated pairs couldn't keep their hands off each other. The fact I couldn't sleep in the same bed as Anevae—be near her every second of the day—made things that much more difficult. The moments I could be near her, I was desperate to be touching her, feeling her skin against mine. If I had it my way, we wouldn't leave her room for days on end because we'd be so wrapped up in each other that the rest of the world didn't matter.

I tried to distract myself before I snatched Anevae and did precisely what I'd been thinking about. Maeyve sat on the couch nearest the window, scarfing down her lunch, and my mind started descending into madness again. We'd shared Anevae the night prior, but I still wasn't convinced that a three-way relationship was sustainable. And adding another person to the mix could mess things up big time.

Anevae stood, staring at me. Her heated gaze stayed focused on me as I approached. "Eat. Your body needs to replenish the energy you used during your lessons."

She clenched her jaw and shook her head, sending crimson-red waves tumbling over her shoulders. When I advanced again, she attempted to step back but found herself pinned between me and the back of the couch.

"You need to eat. I mean it," I said again with a more demanding tone.

Maeyve released a sigh, catching me off guard. "Tell *him* what you want, Anevae. Not me."

Anevae furrowed her brows, and I continued to stare at her expectantly. She didn't respond, so I inched forward until my body was flush against hers. I grabbed the couch on either side of her, boxing her in with a smirk. She wasn't leaving until she answered me...or I moved her.

The scent of her arousal surrounded me, and my cock twitched. It took everything in me not to rip all her clothes off where she stood. But I had to try to control myself.

Anevae sharply inhaled. A jolt of panic shot through me, but her overwhelming arousal replaced it with a fiery need.

"What happened?" I asked, my voice husky with lust.

Be careful about what you project into my mind. I can't always promise I'll be able to keep my hands off you, her smoky voice whispered in my mind.

"Ooh. I almost forgot about this cool little thing we can do. Can I be down in my room and still be able to communicate with you?"

She shrugged.

Hmmm. What you're telling me is that when I'm all alone in my bed, thinking about your pretty pussy, I should show you what I do to quell my desires. Especially when I can't have what I want, I thought. When her heart rate increased, the fiery need coursing through my veins amplified tenfold. I couldn't keep myself from grinding my hips into hers so she could feel my erection. *You have no idea what you do to me; you make me feral. I've never been feral for anything or* anyone *in my life. It's so hard to be close to you and not be inside of you. But you need to eat your lunch, princess.*

When our eyes met, she bit her lip piercing and nodded. I backed away, and she sat down to eat. While she did that, I wandered over to one of the windows so I could readjust myself and put some distance between us.

As I stood staring at the landscape, Cassiel appeared beside me and feigned surprise. "Wow. There isn't much tension surrounding you all for once. That's a miracle."

I snickered. "If you'd shown up about ten minutes ago, that would not have been your reaction. Last night was probably the least amount of tension there's ever been between the three of us, though." The heat of Anevae's gaze bore a hole in me. "Hey, I'm just being honest, princess. Do you want to come over here and give him a sneak peek?"

Throwing her fork down, she stormed over to me and hissed, "Stop egging him on. He's here for a reason. And if you ever want to fuck me again, you will do well not to flaunt what happened between us last night. I know we can trust Cassiel, but there are many others out there that we can't. Our mate status won't stop my grandfather from sentencing you to death if he finds out."

I closed the distance between us and grabbed a handful of her hair, yanking her head back. "We both know that is a complete lie. Just the mention of last night has you ready to go again. You want me just as badly as I want you right now. You forget I can smell it. Now that we're mated, it's like my drug, and I'll never be able to get enough of it." Bending down, I inhaled her intoxicating scent and kissed the exposed skin of her neck, wishing I could sink my teeth into her again. She gasped, and I huffed out a laugh before whispering, "You won't deny me the pleasure of tasting your cunt or your blood because you'd be denying yourself what you want, too. From the moment you saw me this morning, all you could think about was our coupling last night. What was your favorite part? Was it when I licked your sweet pussy? You seemed to really enjoy it when I pounded into you while Maeyve held your hands down for me. What about when I bit you and marked you where no one can see? Out of all of it, I'm betting your favorite was when you rode my cock and made me yours forever. Don't get me wrong, it was fucking hot the way you took over."

Just as I was about to capture her lips, Cassiel cleared his throat. *Damn, angel.*

That snapped Anevae out of the moment, and she released my sides. "Em, let me go, please."

She tried to step away when I loosened my grip on her hair, but I held her close. We stood there, staring at each other for a moment before I finally released her hair. Then, I kissed her and moved to the armchair. She followed shortly after, sitting next to Maeyve on the couch. Cassiel hesitated, staring at us for several minutes, arms piled full of papers and books.

"Cass, are you okay?" Anevae asked.

"I, uh, yes. I'm fine. Sorry," he said as he adjusted everything in his arms, then made his way over to us. Before sitting on the empty couch, he began laying everything out on the table between us.

We all sat there, waiting on bated breath. But when he'd finally separated some of the piles, he looked at Anevae. "I've been trying to avoid talking about this with everyone until I could explain more, but ever since our first skin-to-skin contact, I've been studying a centuries-old prophecy—"

"What does the prophecy say?" Anevae asked.

Maeyve placed her hand on Anevae's leg. "Love, he's trying to tell us. Please let him speak."

Anevae's brows knit together, and her lips pursed, but she let Cassiel continue, "When we were discussing fated mates on your second day of lessons, a prophecy from centuries ago popped into my head. It speaks of a woman who would unite the kingdom as a whole again. This prophecy claims she would be given a fated mate from each territory."

"From *each territory?*" When Cassiel nodded, her eyes grew in size. "I very highly doubt this prophecy would be referring to me. Is it possible that this could be some weird coincidence where I just so happen to have more than one fated mate?"

Cassiel shook his head. "I don't believe it works like that. There's never been a record of any being having more than one fated mate. I also haven't come across a record of same-sex pairings being fated. I've done a bunch of research on the topic since I first met you, looking through all the records I have access to in the library of Baeruil, and I've found no other explanation."

"Fine. Let's entertain the idea that I *am* this woman, and I'm supposed to have *five* mates at once. Emrhys is from Lamatorre, and Cassiel is from Baeruil, but which territory is Maeyve supposed to be from? She's half shifter and half succubus. Could she be my mate from both Kaeuil and Maiviraea? Or would I have two more mates to watch for?"

"This is why I didn't want to discuss it in full with you guys yet. I still don't understand anything beyond what I've told you. I have the original copy written in the ancient language, but the attempts to translate it are disjointed, and there aren't many. I'm trying to find someone who can help without asking too many questions, but it's not common to find someone familiar with the ancient language nowadays."

Shifting in my chair, I added, "I still think it would be a great idea for us to do some research of our own. Maybe there's something you're overlooking that we can find. I'll also look around to see if there's anyone I'm comfortable asking for help." Cassiel glared at me, and I glared right back. "Even you—oh, perfect one—can make mistakes and miss things. Chill your shit. Let's go to the library, ladies."

Chapter Thirty

Anevae

Maeyve, Emrhys, and I spent several hours looking for books that could tell us anything about fated mates. We'd skimmed books in nearly half the library when dinnertime rolled around. We couldn't risk being late, so we rushed to clean up our mess and decide which books to look at in more depth. When we were almost done, Emrhys shooed Maeyve and me away to get ready for dinner. At best, my tardiness would earn me another lecture, and I just couldn't risk drawing any more attention toward myself right now.

Back in my room, we picked out clothes from the armoire and quickly dressed. I was grateful to have Maeyve, who could help me lace up the corset on my dress while I brushed my hair and arranged it to cover the mating mark on my neck.

I was almost done when Emrhys knocked on the door and entered the room. "We only have a few more minutes before we have to be downstairs. Are you ladies almost ready?"

As I ran the brush through the last section of my hair, I said, "I'm all done. Not sure about Maeyve yet."

Maeyve appeared beside me and snorted. "Sweetheart, I've been waiting for you. I'm all set to go."

I set the brush down and approached Emrhys. "You heard her. We're good to go."

With a smirk, I leaned in to give him a quick kiss. He hummed against my lips and tried to grab for me, but I pushed myself from his arms.

"Tease," he muttered.

"Makes it all the better when we get back later," I said as I walked to the door, swaying my hips to remind my mates what they had to look forward to. When I reached the door, I placed my hand on the knob and looked back. "So? Y'all ready or not?"

Both of them hurried to catch up to me, and I laughed. I didn't open the door yet though. "Em, please be careful about how you react while we're around my grandfather. We can't let him suspect something is going on between us."

Emrhys scoffed. "He hasn't even noticed your mating mark from Maeyve yet. And it's on your neck, so it's pretty hard to miss."

"He hasn't noticed that you know of. What if he has but just hasn't said anything yet?" I asked.

"Look, I know your grandfather. If he knew that you two were mated to each other, he would be doing everything in his power to separate you. You may not be full fae, but you're his granddaughter and one of two potential ways for him to ensure the royal line continues. In Caellaias, the first-born male takes over for their parents, but since you don't have a brother, the eldest child is expected to take responsibility. Unless something happens to the eldest child. In your mom's case, her older sister was banished, and everything fell onto her. You're the eldest of his grandchildren—that he knows of, at least. Your aunt hasn't been seen in many years, and it's unknown whether she has children. She has glamour magic, so she could easily hide herself and others amongst the fae. Since you're considered next in line for the throne, he'll be antsy to find out if you have the royal magic. If you do, this kingdom will become yours one day, and your grandfather will expect you to produce heirs. Maeyve is a woman, so she can't help you with that. And I can't guarantee any children we may have will possess magic. He will want you to marry—and mate—a purebred fae," Emrhys explained.

His words sent a shiver through me. There was no hope of me getting to go home because I *did* have glamour magic. "If I tell him I can't harness glamour magic, would he let me go home? If he doesn't think I have that magic, he could see me as useless and unworthy of my royal title."

Emrhys shook his head. "I don't think he'd ever consider you useless or unworthy of a royal title. He just wouldn't rely on you to produce an heir for him. You do have glamour magic, though...right?"

"I do, but I have a very hard time calling it to the surface. I just wonder if my grandfather believes I don't have it if he'd let me go home. What good is a princess—or future queen—who can't produce a suitable heir?"

"Anevae, you're still his granddaughter, and he's not going to let go of you easily. If we're able to, we'll get you home, okay?" Emrhys said sympathetically.

Sighing, I nodded. Maeyve stepped past Emrhys and wrapped me in her arms, trying to help me control my spiraling thoughts.

I love you. Let's get to dinner before your grandfather sends someone after us.

As soon as I entered the dining room, something felt off. My grandfather rose to greet me as he did every evening. When I tried to dodge him, per usual, he grabbed my shoulders and scolded me, "Your attitude *must* improve. I do not appreciate the way you have been acting. When you enter the dining hall, and I rise to greet you, you will not avoid me from here on out. I do not deserve this treatment from you. I have provided you with everything you want and more. I have even gone as far as to let your mutt stay with you—to comfort you during this transition."

Electricity flowed through my body as my magic began to rise, but I fought it back down. I didn't appreciate the way he spoke about my mate, but he was already upset with me, and I didn't want to give him a reason to unleash his anger.

Excitement lit his yellow eyes. "It seems you have been learning to control your magic. This is great news. Have you been able to harness glamour magic yet?"

I shook my head because I knew if I opened my mouth, I wouldn't be able to keep myself from telling him off.

"That's a shame. I will have to discuss your progress with Cassiel tomorrow. Let us get to dinner. I'd like to speak with you and your sister in the sitting room after we have eaten."

After dinner, Aeros and Emrhys escorted us to the sitting room. Our grandfather entered first, sitting in his favorite wingbacked chair while Eiri and I took our spots across from each other. Then, everyone else assumed their positions.

When I chanced a glance at my sister, she looked away from me. It irritated me because things over the last few weeks may have happened very differently if it hadn't been for her. I was also annoyed that I still hadn't been able to ask her about why she'd come to Caellaias if she hadn't been kidnapped. Our grandfather—and Aeros—had worked hard to keep us apart during our supposed free time.

Once everyone was seated, my grandfather took a long breath. "Girls, I wanted to let you know that your parents have finally arrived in Caellaias. I've been keeping tabs on them since they left Eirian's apartment in the human realm, but I also had a sensor placed on all portals to alert me to their arrival. The alarm for this went off early this morning, detecting their presence at the portal in the heart of Baeruil. Now that they know you are both here, my daughter will likely use her glamour magic to get past officials and keep a low profile, so we are on high alert for any level of suspicious activity. What this means for you girls is that, until further notice, you must stay inside the castle. Emrhys, Aeros, keep a close eye on them. If it comes down to it, do not leave their sides. Laeney and Roarc will do anything to get them home. Little do they know, the portals will not allow anyone in this room to pass through it. Even if your mother is able to glamour you all, it will detect your magical signatures, which she cannot alter."

Oh shit. The message I'd scheduled to send to my mom must have been sent. They were coming for us. And now we were all stuck in Caellaias.

Fuck. What have we done? I thought, not sure if either of my mates heard the distress in my thoughts.

Chapter Thirty-One

Maeyve

Anevae's fury and panic filled our bond. It took everything in me not to comfort her, but we were in front of her grandfather, and we needed to be careful about how much affection we showed each other. Looking over at Emrhys, his expression told me he was having the same problem.

"Are you fucking serious?" Anevae roared, voice raw and full of power.

King Casimir's eyes began glowing as he stared his granddaughter down. "Anevae, watch your language. You are a royal, and you must act as such. There are consequences when you do not follow my orders."

Anevae stood with her hands clenched at her sides. Her power was coming to the surface, but she was doing well at holding it back. "If you keep me here against my will, I will fight you every step of the way—fuck the consequences. You're fucking delusional if you think I'm just going to comply with you."

The king laughed, which made Anevae even angrier. "My darling granddaughter, you have no clue what exactly I am capable of. If you do not behave or comply with my orders, I will make your life a living hell. When your mother arrives, ask her what happened when she attempted to disobey me before she left."

"Do you not see a problem with the way you treat others? Because look where your actions have gotten you. All *alone!*"

The king rose and closed the distance between him and Anevae. Lightning surrounded his hands. "You will do well to watch your mouth. If you speak out of turn again and do not show me the respect I deserve, I will not hesitate to punish you. Maybe I'll start by separating you from your pet."

My heart beat frantically, fearing the worst as I processed the king's threats. *Anevae, don't do something you'll regret. We can talk about this later. We don't want to get on his bad side,* I pleaded through our bond.

Huffing out a breath, she took a step back and stood down. I allowed my relief to wash through the bond.

The lightning engulfing the king's hands dissipated as his composure returned. With a smile, he said, "Right, well. Off you all go. I will see you tomorrow."

Thank fuck, Anevae said through the bond as she turned and stormed out of the room.

Rushing to my feet, I followed her back to our suite. The moment she was inside, she was attempting to rip off her dress again.

"For fuck's sake, Anevae! You're going to ruin another dress," I hissed as I threw the door closed behind me.

Her eyes glowed with a pattern I hadn't seen yet—the blue of her eyes had intensified with the addition of tiny red specks. When she spoke, her voice deepened a touch. "I don't fucking *care.* He cannot control me; I refuse to let him. I'm not this puppet that he can do what he pleases with."

"Sweetheart, I understand he's pushing your buttons, but remember he has his own agenda. He doesn't care what *you* want or how he treats you; it's all about what *he* wants. That's how it's been for over two centuries. No one challenges his decisions—ever. The last person to defy him was your mother. I can't imagine that her return will be pleasant."

After a moment of quiet contemplation, she grunted and turned around so I could untie her dress. Just as the fabric slid from her body, Cassiel appeared before her.

"Are you—? Oh. I'm so sorry," he said as he averted his gaze.

"I'm not sure I like that you can randomly appear wherever you like without warning. Now, you get to torture yourself. I will not cover myself just to make you comfortable. You should've thought about that before you appeared in *my* bedroom." She stepped out of the puddle of fabric at her feet and climbed on the bed—almost like she was showing herself off to him. Of course, it was the one day she decided not to wear underwear.

"Gods damn it," Cassiel muttered, still trying to keep his eyes from roaming over her exposed body.

I was tempted to crawl on the bed with her and tease Cassiel but decided against it...for the time being. Instead, I picked up Anevae's dress, depositing it into the laundry before taking a seat on the couch. Cassiel continued to stand there awkwardly, seemingly unsure of what to do.

"Well, can I do something for you, Cassiel?" Anevae asked with a sultry undertone to her voice.

"I just came to make sure you were alright."

"You've established that I'm not under distress, so why are you still here?"

Finally, he met her gaze. "Just because you are not under physical distress does not mean you are not under mental or emotional distress that I cannot sense. I heard about what happened after dinner this evening and wanted to make sure you were okay. Would you rather I leave and act as if I don't care?"

"Sorry. I'm fine, I guess. Nothing I can't deal with on my own right now," she said quietly as she pulled a blanket on to cover herself.

"Anevae, I'm sorry. I —"

"It's fine, Cassiel. I wasn't exactly polite to you either."

"I shouldn't have snapped at you like that, though. I just want to be able to help you if I can."

"My parents are in Caellaias, and I led them here. To make matters worse, my grandfather has blocked all of the portals for my family; we can't return to the human realm for the foreseeable future."

"Where did they come through?" Cassiel asked.

"According to my grandfather, they came in through a portal in Baeruil."

Cassiel's expression turned hopeful. "I can help them get to safety. I can be the link between you and your parents. I could—"

Anevae shook her head and interrupted Cassiel again, "No. The king is keeping tabs on them. I don't want you to get stuck in the middle of this mess. It'd almost be better for them to be at the castle anyway."

Walking to the bed, he placed his massive hands on the footboard. "You are my fated mate. I will do anything I can to make you happy. If that means inserting myself in a complicated situation, I'll gladly do it. Now that I have you, I will never stray far from you."

Anevae's eyes dropped as she asked, "What if I'm actually able to go back to the human realm?"

"I will go *anywhere* as long as I am with you. You could drag me into the depths of Kaeuil, and I would suffer through it all if it kept us together."

Anevae looked up to meet Cassiel's gaze again. A tense silence stretched across the room, but then a knock sounded on the door.

Chapter Thirty-Two

Emrhys

Silence greeted me as I approached Anevae's bedroom door. I stood there for another minute and still didn't hear anything, so I knocked. Immediately, shuffling and whispers were coming from inside. I was about to knock again, but then the door cracked open. Looking inside, one of Anevae's blue eyes found mine, and a look of relief washed over her face.

"Thank fuck it's just you," she said as she opened the door to let me in. Her creamy, pale skin was on full display without an inch of clothing to cover her.

I hurried into the room, slamming the door behind me. "What do you mean 'just me?' Why are you answering the door naked anyway?"

Anevae crossed her arms over her full breasts with a satisfied look on her face. "I was teaching Cass here a lesson."

My eyes trailed down her body, admiring every inch—every curve, dimple, stretch mark, freckle...my mating mark on her breast. The lower my eyes got, the harder my cock grew. Fuck she was beautiful. I wanted to have my hands all over her. "If I may ask, what kind of lesson were you trying to teach him? I feel like I need this kind of lesson, too, especially if it keeps you naked. It makes it that much more likely that I get to worship your body the way it deserves. What did the big softie do to make him deserve one of these torturous lessons?"

Cassiel shifted uncomfortably near the bed, trying incredibly hard to look anywhere but Anevae's naked physique. I couldn't keep the lopsided grin off my face.

"He conveyed himself into my room while I was getting undressed. Now, he's learning why he shouldn't do that. You've already had a lesson similar to this. Remember when you walked in here before knocking? When Maeyve and I were...busy?"

An image from that night popped into my head, and my cock twitched. "Ah damn. That was rough. I was so desperate for a release—" I stopped. *Shit. I wasn't sure how she would react if I told her I'd had sex with someone else or if it was even something I should worry about. At the time, we weren't even acknowledging each other, but I knew we couldn't deny the pull we felt between us.*

Anevae's jaw clenched and unclenched. After letting out a long breath, she said, "Go ahead. Say it out loud so everyone else can hear it, too."

My cheeks reddened. I'd accidentally projected my thoughts through our bond. "I was so desperate to get you off my mind that night that I went to the brothel in Kanlyrae. I thought you hated me—thought you'd never want me. I had to find a way not to feel anything for you. If it makes you feel any better, it didn't help at all."

"I mean, I guess I understand. It doesn't make it any easier to hear, though. I wanted you...even when I hated you, but I knew you were trying to do what you thought was right."

"I'm sorry," I whispered.

"It's fine. Really. It couldn't have been easy for you to watch me with Maeyve when I know what you feel for me now."

"It wasn't. And I know I've said it a million times, but being so close that I could touch you, it hurts not to have you wrapped up in my arms or pinned beneath me. I imagine it's a million times worse for Cassiel. Please put some clothes on before one of us does as we please with you."

Every word that left my lips had her arousal rising, and it was getting increasingly more difficult to resist going to her. When I tried to avert my gaze, she approached me.

"You're making this nearly impossible," I said.

A smirk appeared on her lips as she placed her hands on my chest. "Should we give Cass a show? You and Maeyve can dominate me like you did the other night. Or would you rather watch Cassiel fuck me first, then you can have your turn? Or, Maeyve can please me while you both sit on the couch, stroking your cocks as you watch me come."

A growl rumbled low in my chest as I grabbed her wrist. The effects of the bond spread up my arm, and I shivered. "Anevae, watch that mouth. If you don't back up in the next few seconds, I won't be able to contain myself any longer."

Pouting, she said, "But what if that's what I want?"

The tiny shred of self-restraint I had snapped, and I lifted her, throwing her down on the bed and pinning her hands above her head so she was on full display. A gasp left her at the impact, and she stared up at me wide-eyed.

Grinding into her, I said, "Remember who you're playing this game with. Cassiel and I are already risking our lives for you. It's killing me not to nestle into your sweet body and make you come all over my cock, again and again. Fuck. Just the thought of that makes me never want to leave this room."

Even though I was pinning her down, she lifted her head and claimed my mouth. Against my better judgment, I kissed her back. Her lips parted, and she slid her tongue out to caress mine. I gripped her hands tighter and ground into her again on instinct, dying to bury myself inside her tight pussy. She moaned into my mouth and, through our bond, said, *Then don't. My grandfather said you were to stay with me, no matter what, to make sure I was safe. Stay with me, Em.*

I let out a small groan as I pushed myself off her and rose from the bed, breathing heavily. She looked positively fuckable lying on that bed, and it was dangerous. "You know this isn't wise."

She shrugged as I came to a stop beside Cassiel. His gaze was fixed on the floor, trying to keep his eyes off her, but he was failing miserably. Finally, he said, "Anevae, I need to leave before I make a huge mistake."

Anevae crawled off the bed and sauntered toward him. The way she swayed her hips had us all mesmerized.

When she reached the angel, she took a fist full of his shirt and yanked him down to her level. "I'm tired of fighting this bond. For whatever reason, we were meant to be mated to one another. Get on this bed and claim me like I know you want to."

I wasn't sure who moved first, but their lips collided in a messy kiss, and he wrapped his arms around her, pulling her to him. She wrapped her legs around his waist and loosened her grip on his shirt. With a few long strides, he laid her on the bed and said, "I've never..."

Flabbergasted, I blurted, "You mean to tell me in all the years you've been alive, you've *never* had sex before?"

Anevae turned to me with a smirk on her face. "You want to show him how it's done then, Em? Show him what I like and how to make me scream."

My cock twitched at the suggestion, and I was by her side in seconds. "You don't have to ask me twice, princess. First, I'd like to taste that delicious cunt. Maybe Maeyve can ride your face at the same time."

Anevae returned to kissing Cassiel, and I glanced to where Maeyve sat on the couch, thighs clenched together. Her sweet scent surrounded me, mingling with Anevae's, and I had to bite my lip to stifle a moan. They both smelled so delectable. "Would you like to ride our mate's face, Maeyve?" She nodded, and I said, "Cassiel, why don't you get our girl ready for us? It's going to be a long night, but I know how much she wants us. Our needy girl can take it all."

I wandered toward the sink, taking my time undressing, but the small moans escaping from my mate's pouty pink lips had me growing more and more desperate to be inside her. When my last article of clothing hit the floor, I splashed some water on my face and then walked around the bed. Cassiel was kissing down Anevae's neck to her breast—toward my mating mark. It reminded me that soon, she'd also be his. As he reached her nipple, he circled it with his tongue, and she arched her back.

Leaning down, I ran my fingers through her hair as he continued kissing down her body. "You make such beautiful sounds for us. I can't wait to taste you again. Should I bite your clit this time? My fang barely scraped it last time, and you were ready to fly off this bed."

Cassiel kissed her hip as the words left my lips. Her eyes grew wide, and she inhaled sharply. *You wouldn't.*

I rounded the bed, taunting her as Cassiel climbed off. *Oh, but I would. The taste of your blood and cunt together. That sounds heavenly.* I stood next to Cassiel and looked at Maeyve—now completely undressed. Cassiel moved to the foot of the bed and grasped the footboard.

Eyes hooded with lust, Anevae met Cassiel's hungry gaze and said, "Take your cock out and stroke it while you watch Em eat me out. I want to see how hard you are for me—how desperate you are to be inside me."

Cassiel groaned and gripped the footboard so hard his knuckles were turning white.

Anevae trailed her hand down her body, dipping it between her thighs, and played with herself while we all watched. "Please, baby," she whispered.

"Fuck. You're so gods damned gorgeous," he said as he tore his hands from the footboard and reached for his trousers.

Still playing with herself, Anevae bit her lip piercing before praising Cassiel, "Such a good boy." When his cock sprung free, though, the heat in her eyes intensified. "Fuck. Maybe I should've ridden you while I sucked off Em. But I want our first time to be you and me since you've never done this."

Cassiel palmed his length and trailed his eyes down her body, stopping at where her hand was hidden between her thighs. She spread her legs open wider so he could see her wet pussy. A breathy moan left her lips as she rubbed her clit and watched Cassiel stroke himself.

Maeyve climbed on the bed beside her and began kissing her deeply. When their tongues tangled, she pinched Anevae's nipples lightly. I wrapped my hand loosely around my shaft, enjoying the view before me.

After a few minutes, I climbed onto the bed between Anevae's legs and kissed up her thigh. The scent of her arousal consumed me. *Gods, you smell so good,* I said through our bond. When I reached the top of her thigh, I pulled her hand to my mouth and licked her fingers clean.

Maeyve sat up and looked down at Anevae. "Are you ready, love?"

"More so than I ever have been," Anevae said, voice husky with need.

"Perfect. Maeyve, sit facing me. I want you to play with her nipples while you ride her face," I said, settling into my spot between her legs.

"You heard him. Come over here so I can lick that pretty pussy," Anevae said.

Maeyve straddled her face, trying to hover. But Anevae was having none of that, pulling Maeyve flush against her tongue. Maeyve's gasp quickly turned to a moan as she settled. Her hands found Anevae's nipples and tweaked them to sharp points. I spent a second watching them, and then I licked up Anevae's wet slit.

Her body tensed, so I sent my reassurances through the bond: *Show Cass how perfect you look when you come undone on my tongue.* Then, I sucked her clit into my mouth, rolling it around on my tongue. She let out a muffled cry, and I laughed. *So eager to come all over my face are we? We've only just begun.*

It just feels so fucking good when you fuck me with your tongue.

Within mere minutes, she was a shaking mess. Her legs were around my neck as I drank up her essence like it was the only sustenance I'd ever need. And when she came, her screams were lost to Maeyve's cunt.

When Anevae's legs loosened around my neck, I untangled myself from her body and shifted onto my knees, admiring the sight before me. Anevae's nails dug into Maeyve's thighs, nearly breaking the skin as she devoured Maeyve. Maeyve's gaze was on Anevae's breasts, but her hands had stopped moving. She was hardly able to focus as she let out moans that were all too quiet. I placed a finger under her chin and encouraged her to look up at me. When she did, I moved my hand to the nape of her neck and grabbed a handful of her hair, yanking her head back further.

Then, I did something I'd wanted to do for weeks: I captured her lips with mine, sliding my tongue into her mouth so she could taste our mate. As we kissed, I nestled my cock into Anevae's entrance. She immediately wrapped her legs around my waist, trying to impale herself on my rigid length.

Patience, princess. You're going to get plenty of pleasure this evening. Make the little fox scream.

Anevae's grip on Maeyve tightened as she buried her face deeper in Maeyve's cunt. Maeyve threw her head back further, breaking our kiss, and cried out. At the same time, she pinched Anevae's nipples. The movement pushed my tip just inside Anevae, but it was withdrawn before I could do anything.

Emrhys, please. I need you inside me, Anevae begged.

You're being such a good girl, telling me what you need. Should I be nice and give it to you? I asked as I let go of Maeyve's hair and moved both hands down to her hips, pushing her harder against Anevae's tongue.

Emrhys, ple— Anevae began, but I sheathed myself inside her, effectively cutting off her plea.

Tell me what you want me to do, I said as I pulled out of her.

Fuck me like this is the last time you'll ever get to touch me.

Sliding back into her slowly, I said, *If this were the last time I'd ever get to touch you, I'd take my time with you. I know that's not what you want, so try again.*

I want it fast and hard. Show me no mercy.

A small laugh escaped my lips, and I did as she requested, pistoning my hips to pound into her. Her walls clamped around my cock, coaxing me closer and closer to my orgasm. When Maeyve's moans grew louder and more strained, I knew she was close to coming, too. Leaning forward, I kissed her lips once, then kissed across her jaw to her neck.

I'm going to bite Maeyve, and when I do, she's going to come hard. Get ready, princess, I warned Anevae.

Reaching Maeyve's shoulder, I kissed it, then ran my tongue up to her ear. I nipped the lobe before taking it lightly between my front teeth. When I released it, I whispered, "Come all over our mate's face, beautiful. Ride her until your legs can't handle it anymore."

"Bite me."

I kissed back down her neck, taking my time. "Mmm. Now you're asking for it. I was going to do it either way."

Her pulse quickened as I reached the top of her shoulder again. I placed one more kiss on her skin before sinking my teeth into her flesh. The scream that came from her was one that I'd have been able to hear clear across the castle. Retracting my fangs, I let her blood flow freely into my mouth. It was surprisingly sweet, like berries, even though succubus blood was usually bitter.

I moved my hands from Maeyve's hips to her ass when she began shaking, lifting her off Anevae's face and pulling her to me. Not only did it allow me to hear them both continue to make intoxicating sounds, but I got to feel their bare skin against mine at the same time.

Maeyve's arms wrapped around my neck as she tangled one hand into my hair. I took a short pull of her blood, and she pulled the strands lightly. When I took a longer pull, her head fell back further, and her grip on my hair tightened.

I was getting so close.

As I continued drinking Maeyve's blood little by little, my thrusts into Anevae's pussy grew frenzied. Anevae's screams grew louder, and her walls clamped tightly around my cock. She was getting close, but I was seconds from exploding, so I maneuvered one hand between us and began working her clit. That was all it took for her to come tumbling over the edge, pulling me right along with her.

I gave us all a moment before lifting my mouth from Maeyve's shoulder to nick my lip and heal her. Then, I cleaned any remaining blood up and let her go. She flopped down beside Anevae on the bed for a moment before kissing her and heading toward the bath.

Below me, Anevae was still breathing hard with her eyes closed. She looked so beautiful, with her crimson waves spread around her head and her face a mess. I leaned down to lick up some of Maeyve's arousal and gave Anevae a deep kiss as I eased out of her.

"She tastes almost as good as you. Now, it's the big guy's turn. I'm going to get Maeyve and myself all washed up so you guys can have some space." Then, I gave her nose a quick kiss and climbed off the bed to join Maeyve.

Chapter Thirty-Three

Cassiel

My gaze never left Anevae, no matter what else was happening. I wanted to focus on her—see what she liked and how she reacted to certain things. As she grew closer to climax, I tightened my hand around my shaft and increased the pace of my strokes. I was so close to orgasm.

The moment Emrhys pulled Maeyve to him, Anevae's eyes were on me. Her heated gaze was almost enough for me to come alone, but I held on; I wanted to wait until I was inside her.

Growing up, I'd always been told sex was ceremonial for angels. It was only done to bring in a new generation by those hand-picked by the elders. It wasn't common because angels could live for thousands of years; Baeruil was always fairly calm. It was a land of peace, for the most part.

Anevae's screams pulled me from my thoughts, and I knew she was there. It took everything in me to keep from crashing over the edge with her. Releasing my cock, I gripped the edge of the bed instead. I stood there, watching her body tremble with pleasure.

When Maeyve collapsed on the bed next to Anevae, I ripped my hands from the footboard and fixed my clothes. Then, I turned toward the couches. I wasn't sure I could do it. I wanted her so badly I ached, but I worried I'd do something wrong. If we did this and we mated, I would be sentencing myself to death. Just because I'd already lived a long time didn't mean I was ready to give it all up. My mind kept telling me I needed to do more research on the prophecy, but my heart said fuck it all and take what's mine.

As I stood looking at the fireplace, Anevae walked up behind me and wrapped her arms around my middle. "What's wrong?"

"It's nothing," I said as my cock twitched.

"Talk to me, Cass."

"It's fine. I should really get going."

"Not before you fuck me into oblivion."

"Anevae, we don't want—"

Unclasping her hands, she came around to stand before me. She was still completely naked, and I wanted nothing more than to bury myself in her, but this was all foreign to me. And I was a little scared that I'd somehow fuck everything up or the king would discover our secrets.

"I know for a fact you didn't come, even though you likely wanted to more than once." Reaching down, she opened my trousers and slipped her hand onto my needy cock. Wrapping her hand around it, she stroked me from root to tip once before running her thumb over my tip, collecting the pre-cum I hadn't wiped up. Slipping her hand out, she brought her thumb to her mouth, sucking it in. After pulling it out with a pop, she said, "I know you're scared, but I want this; I want all three of you. Whatever this prophecy may say, I don't care right now. I'm fated to you all. We'll figure it out at some point, but now is not the time."

My hands were clenched at my sides, still stuck on what to do. She placed her hands on my chest and took another step in, almost flush against me.

Getting on her tiptoes, she gave me a chaste kiss. The momentary contact lit a fire under my skin, and that was it. I ripped my shirt off and threw it on the floor. The next second, I lifted Anevae into my arms, and she wrapped her legs around my middle. Pants slowly falling off, I walked her over to the bed and laid her down. I kicked the fabric off at my feet and repositioned myself between her legs.

Placing my hands on either side of her head, I kissed her. "Are you sure you want to do this?"

An intense fire burned in the red flecks of her blue eyes as she stared back at me. Before I knew what was happening, she had me on my back, the tip of my dick nestled at her entrance.

She was strong. Seeing the red in her eyes made me wonder if it was her wolf trying to come out to play. It would explain how she was able to flip me over so easily.

"I want you beside me. Through the good, the bad, and the ugly. I'd love to see my grandfather try to separate any of you three from me. You're *mine.*"

After the last word left her sweet lips, she impaled herself on me. Even though Emrhys had just been inside her, she threw her head back to let herself adjust to my size. From the little I'd seen of Emrhys' dick, he was on the thicker side, but I was at least an inch longer. When she sat up fully, I went deeper. Her sharp inhale told me the angle had either hurt or felt good, but I wasn't sure which.

"We can—" I started.

"Do not say we can stop. You feel so fucking good. I haven't ridden a guy as long as you in a while. Just give me a second, please."

I trailed my hands up her thighs to her hips. "Whatever you need. If you w—"

Mid-sentence, she smiled down at me, slowly lifting herself off my throbbing cock before coming back down hard. I grunted as I grabbed her hips. Gods, she was so wet, slick with her arousal and Emrhys' cum.

I wanted *more*.

As if she could read my mind, she leaned forward, putting her hands on my chest. Her hair cascaded over her shoulders, almost long enough to touch the bed. Rocking her hips, she slid all the way up my shaft until the tip was barely inside her and then back down until I was fully seated. A shaky breath left me as she moved to do it again.

"Do you like that, baby?" she asked, her voice husky with need.

"Yes," I panted.

"Do you want me to do anything different? Did you like it better when I was sitting up? Your cock rubbed perfectly against my G-spot when I did that. But I want you to come in my pretty pussy. Tell me what you want."

"I-I don't know, but this feels so fucking amazing."

After a small laugh—which caused her to clench tight around my dick and me to groan—she continued. Her quiet moans told me she wasn't getting close, but she was enjoying herself.

"Go faster. I want you to get there, too," I said, shifting my hands to her breasts, which were swaying in my face. I swept my thumbs over the strange jewelry that adorned her nipples, and she rolled her lip between her teeth, slowing down.

I pinched the stiff peaks lightly, and her eyes swept back down to my face. "I didn't say you could slow down. I asked you to go faster. Now, ride me, or I will flip you onto your back and do as *I* please with *you*."

Grinning, she rocked her hips slowly. I pinched her nipples harder, and she sped up. As a reward, I traded my fingers for my mouth, sucking a nipple in and swirling my tongue around the pebbled flesh.

When I released her nipple, I whispered, "That's a good girl."

Her nails dug into my chest as she quickened her pace. But it wasn't enough for her. She dropped her hands to the bed, bringing her lips that much closer. Gripping her sides, I listened to my instincts and pounded into her from below, synchronizing with her every movement.

"Fuck," I muttered, unsure if I could form a complete thought to save my life. After licking my lips, I tried to kiss her, but she was just out of reach. "Kiss me."

Her lips came down hard on mine, claiming me with one kiss alone. Our lips parted, and I slid my tongue out to caress hers. It was an evening full of firsts, and I wouldn't have changed it for a thing.

Continuing my thrusts into her, I knew I wouldn't be able to last much longer. Watching her with the other two had already gotten me close. Sex was still foreign to me, but being with her felt natural...perfect. I never wanted to leave this moment.

When her lips left mine, she kissed across my jaw to my neck and bit me playfully. "I'm dying to mark you. I want you to have no doubt in your mind that you're mine, and I'm yours."

There was a stutter in my thrusting as I took in what she said. Mark me? Like she'd done to Maeyve? Had she marked Emrhys? Shifters and vampires mated by marking, but I wasn't sure how angels mated. What if she started the mating process, and I didn't know how to finish it? Would I be able to withstand that?

"Relax, Cass. I won't do it unless you want me to," she whispered in my ear.

Realizing we'd both stopped moving, I said, "I'm sorry. I don't know how angels mate, and that makes me nervous. If you bite me..."

"Do what feels natural to you. That's how I mated with Maeyve. It was an accident, but it was meant to happen." Sighing, she pushed up to look me in the eyes. "Don't worry about how it will happen; don't overthink this. Focus on us, on how good it feels to have my wet cunt squeezing your cock, coaxing you to your climax."

With a groan, I nodded and pulled her back in for another kiss. When our lips met, I flipped her over so I was on top again, pinning her down. A small laugh escaped her, and she wrapped her arms around my neck. I withdrew from her slowly before thrusting into her hard, then continuing that pattern.

Breaking our kiss, she pleaded, "Faster."

When I increased my pace, her breathing grew more ragged, bringing her closer to her release. I was right there with her, my whole body on fire—desperation winning out.

"I'm not going to last much longer," I said breathlessly.

"I'm almost there. Don't stop. Please."

After a few more thrusts, I spilled into her, unable to hold it back. Anevae was right behind me, crying out her release as her pussy milked my dick, trying to get every last drop of my cum into her.

Chapter Thirty-Four

Maeyve

When I climbed off the bed, I headed straight for the bath. My thighs were soaking wet, and I needed to clean myself up. But as I inched away from the bed, my shoulder began aching. What the hell had I done to irritate it?

Shrugging it off, I started the water, trying not to make it too hot. Emrhys walked up behind me and wrapped his arms around my middle as I stood. He pulled me into him, his still-hard cock pressing into my ass, and then kissed my shoulder. Sparks shot through my body, and I ripped myself from his grip.

Eyes wide, he stood there staring at me. "What the fuck was that? You just let me bite you, but I can't hold you?"

"Did you not feel that? That...spark?"

"I didn't feel a damn thing."

"Wh-when you kissed my shoulder, there was this—like—spark that shot through my whole body. You seriously didn't feel it?"

Raising an eyebrow, he shook his head. Neither of us moved until I realized the water was still running. Emrhys moved to shut it off before I could. I took a step toward the sink, and the ache in my shoulder intensified. Hissing, I reached up to touch the spot. The puncture marks there hadn't healed, and the wound was extremely inflamed.

"What did you do to my shoulder, Emrhys? It's like super inflamed and achy. I've never had this happen when I've been bitten in the past."

Going on the defense, he crossed his arms over his chest. "I didn't do anything except bite you. And I healed it with my own blood."

"You clearly didn't heal it if it's like this."

He shifted uncomfortably on his feet. "Bites are always a little inflamed for a bit, but it's not bleeding anymore. That happens sometimes. What do you mean it's achy?"

"I mean that it's fucking aching. I've never had a vampire bite affect me like this. They've always just closed up and healed within minutes."

"And how long has it been since a vampire has bitten you?" he asked, a smugness in his tone.

"It's been a bit, but that doesn't mean I don't remember."

"Maeyve, come on. Let's talk about this later. We need to get cleaned up," he said, reaching out for me.

Scowling at him, I took a step forward and took his hand. A tingling sensation spread up my arm, and I jumped. My eyes widened as I refocused on his ruby-red eyes.

"There's no fucking way," I whispered.

"Did I..." he started, but trailed off. Clearing his throat, he gripped my hand tighter. "Did I start a mating bond between us?"

"That's impossible. We're both..."

"We're both already mated to Anevae. But her bonds are different as they are; why wouldn't ours be, too? I just don't know what to do. What does this mean for us? How will this affect us all?"

He tried to loosen his grip—to pull away from me— and I tightened my hold on him. Yanking him to me, I wrapped my arms around his neck. "Let's take a page out of Anevae's book for once: everything happens for a reason. Don't run away from this. Let's just embrace it."

Clenching his jaw, he placed his hands on my hips. "Bite me then. I'm hesitant to go through with this but fuck if I'm not curious. Let's see what happens."

"I'm not going to fucking do this for pure fun. You know, just for the heck of it. I refuse to let myself follow you like some love-sick puppy."

I squeaked as he lifted me off my feet and slammed my back against the wall, erection pressed into my wet center as he held me up.

"Do you think I touched you—*bit you*—for pure fucking fun? Do you think I still have a hard-on just because of the sounds coming from Anevae? I'm fucking attracted to *you*, too, Maeyve. I think you're gorgeous and funny, but you're also stubborn and a huge pain in my ass. Everything with Anevae would have been so much easier if you hadn't been around, but like Anevae, and now you have said, everything happens for a reason. Bite me. I will not let you suffer this whole thing out. Anevae would hate me...I would hate myself."

I continued staring at him for another minute, contemplating what I wanted to do. We were both tied to Anevae; this was just an additional bond. She'd already mated with each of us separately, and nothing happened there. What was to say that it couldn't be like that with Emrhys and me? He'd already started the bond. It was just up to me to finish it.

"Take us into the bath before all that warm water goes to waste," I said.

Emrhys raised an eyebrow and started to protest, but when I clenched my jaw, he thought better of it. As soon as he stepped in, he tried to put me down, but I just shook my head at him. He raised his eyebrow again, asking the question in his mind without even opening his mouth.

"Sit," I demanded.

Again, he hesitated, but I pursed my lips to show him I was serious, and he sat, still holding me. When he settled, he released me, but I didn't move off him. Instead, I nestled his cock at my entrance and smiled.

I swept my fingers across his shoulders and bit my lip, contemplating whether I wanted to be honest with him. When I trailed them back to the base of his skull, I tangled my hands in his hair again. "You know, I haven't been with a man in over fifty years—since before my escape from Maiviraea."

"And you're going to let me be the first one? How lucky am I?" he asked, his voice full of his usual sarcasm.

I rolled my eyes and gave him a fake laugh, tugging at his hair. "Don't ruin this. Just sit here like a good boy—"

"Oooh. Now you're giving me orders? Sweetheart, I think you know that won't go well with me. If it weren't for the fact you need to bite me, I'd have you bent over the edge of this tub, showing you who's the one in charge here."

Smirking, I slid down his shaft, inch by inch. The further down I got, the harder I dug my nails into his shoulders. He was so thick, and it'd been so gods damned long.

He threw his back with a hiss. "Fuck, and I thought Anevae was tight. You're not going to be able to seat yourself fully without getting hurt."

"I'll get used to it in a moment. Just...don't move."

Bringing his hands back down on my hips, he nodded but didn't move otherwise. I worked myself up and down his length slowly, pushing myself further with every stroke until he was buried to the hilt inside me. Not daring to stop, I leaned forward to kiss his exposed neck.

"Fuck, Maeyve. You're so fucking tight."

I continued rocking my hips as I kissed down his neck to his shoulder—the one Anevae had marked only one day before. Kissing it, I moved to the other side. Anevae would be the angel on one shoulder, while I would be his personal devil on the other. His hands gripped my hips tighter, trying not to move. Just to drive him crazy, I slowed my movements. His groan told me it was working.

"It's only been a couple of minutes. We can't let you get there quite yet, can we?" I teased.

He groaned again. "I'm trying, but you're so tight and clearly know what you're doing. Do you know how hard it is not to take over?"

With a breathy laugh against his skin, I said, "Hmm. It sounds like you prefer to dominate; I'm going to have to break you of that. Both Anevae and I like to switch it up every once in a while. Maybe we can dominate you together. Wouldn't that be fun?"

"*That* I might like."

"I'll keep that in mind for the next time we all have a free moment together." Starting to get closer, I said, "Rub my clit."

He moved his hand down and pressed his thumb to my clit, putting delicious amounts of friction against my aching flesh. As I rode him harder and faster, I nipped playfully at his neck and shoulder until we were both on the brink of orgasm when I finally bit him.

Chapter Thirty-Five

Anevae

Cassiel and I got cleaned up and settled on the couch across from Maeyve and Emrhys, who sat together. They were even more comfortable with each other after their bath. Something more seemed to have changed between them, but I couldn't decipher what it was.

After I stared at Maeyve for what must have been an inappropriate amount of time, her voice slid into my head, *Somehow, Emrhys and I are also mated. We initiated a bond with each other, even though we're mated to you.*

I think you're telling the wrong person, sweetheart, Emrhys' voice was in my mind, too.

Wait. Why can I hear you both talking to each other through our bond? You two can hear each other? I asked, not sure if they'd know the answer themselves.

You heard me? Emrhys asked, eyes wide.

I pursed my lips and scowled at Emrhys. *If I hadn't, would I have asked the question?*

Maeyve narrowed her eyes at me. "We're learning a whole lot of new things with these bonds. This could be a whole lot of fun if we add Cassiel into the mix. Should Emrhys and I bite him now, or does he want to miss out on all the fun?"

Cassiel raised a brow and asked, "Can someone explain, please?"

With a sigh, I shot a dirty look at Maeyve. "Since I've mated with them, I've been able to communicate with them separately through a telepathic bond. Well, now Maeyve and Emrhys have mated, too, and our communication thread seems to be between the three of us. Basically, they're saying they'd like you to be a part of it."

When I looked back at Cassiel, his brows were furrowed. Without looking away, I told the other two, *Not yet. Give him some time. This is all a shock to him. Plus, I haven't bitten him yet; we're not mated.*

Why not? Maeyve asked.

We don't know how angels mate. I don't want to start a bond we don't know how to complete, I explained.

I guess that makes sense, Emrhys said.

"Anyway, it's getting pretty late. We should all head to bed," I said, ending the conversation between my mates and me.

Cassiel was the first to rise, kissing me on my forehead and then turning to the others. "Have a good evening. I'll see you all in the morning." After a short bow, he was gone.

"Having sex with him and not completing that bond is going to take a toll on you both. I hope you know that," Emrhys said.

Glaring daggers at him, I said, "And what would you know about that? We know what we've gotten ourselves into."

Emrhys approached me, concern evident on his face. "I just want you to be careful. If you don't watch out, one of you will lose control in the worst possible way, likely blowing our cover. We can't have that, and you know it."

I stood, pointed my finger at his chest, and said, "We are handling this the best way we know how. You weren't much fucking help earlier. You encouraged us to have sex without even considering what could happen."

"You started this entire thing and didn't stop it either!" he hissed as he stepped into my finger. "You went right on through with it. None of us knew the consequences if you had sex with him. Every single one of us could have stopped it, but we didn't. I'm just trying to watch out for everyone involved, especially you."

I let out an exasperated sigh. "I'm going to bed. I'm tired. Good night, Em."

When I stepped past him, he grabbed my arm and pulled me back to him.

Staring at the floor, I said, "I'm not up for this right now. Everything was amazing tonight until now. I won't argue with you about what we should have done or what *might* happen."

"I'm sorry," he whispered. Releasing my arm, he brought his hand up to grip my chin. Urging me to look at him, he continued, "I want to kiss you because we never know when we'll get to do it again."

I met his gaze and nodded before I placed my hand on his chest. Then I rose to my toes and kissed him lightly. "Good night, Em. I'll see you in the morning."

"I'll see you in the morning. Sleep well."

***

Lessons over the next few days were rough. None of us wanted to keep our hands off each other, but we had to maintain a certain facade so my grandfather didn't suspect anything was going on. Emrhys was the dutiful guard, keeping a close eye on me as he'd been instructed to. Cassiel was the proper teacher my grandfather expected him to be. And Maeyve—well, Maeyve was being her usual, ornery self.

Maeyve and Emrhys helped me as much as they could, reading every book about fated mates available to us in Castle Rilvara. The information we gleaned from those accompanied the information Cassiel was able to get from the library in Baeruil.

Cassiel spent most of his time trying to figure out how angels mated. Because angels weren't supposed to have fated mates, finding anything on the matter was nearly impossible. Every time he was near me, all he wanted to do was touch me, and it irritated him greatly. The physical ache we both experienced to be near one another could be alleviated if we mated—I'd proven that when I mated both Emrhys and Maeyve. The problem was that if I started the mating bond with Cassiel and we couldn't figure out how to complete it, we'd become increasingly desperate for each other.

With each passing day, I agonized over my parents' arrival. It'd already been several days, and my grandfather hadn't given us any updates on their whereabouts. I wasn't sure how long it took to travel from the portal in Baeruil to Castle Rilvara, but I knew they'd be arriving any day. Cassiel's offer to help my parents replayed in my mind whenever I thought about them and I started to regret refusing his help. Their arrival wouldn't be pleasant, but I hoped my grandfather wouldn't be too harsh.

Sitting on the couch beside Maeyve one day, I glanced at both of my men. They were positioned on either side of the couch across from me, noses buried in books, doing research. I was supposed to be helping, but I couldn't help myself; they were both so damned stunning in their own way. I wanted to crawl into the space between them and snuggle into their warmth, to touch their skin and feel the comforting tingling that meant they were real.

Not only were they real, they were *mine*.

I still wasn't sure it was enough to make me stay in Caellaias, though. At some point, I could've had the chance to go home, and I was uncertain if I would take it or stay with my mates. They said they'd come with me, but I didn't want them to abandon everything they knew. One thing I was certain of was that I couldn't live under my grandfather's thumb for the rest of my life. Ultimately, I'd cross that bridge when we got there.

Chapter Thirty-Six

Emrhys

We settled into a new groove after a couple of weeks. Each day, we would wake up, eat a quick breakfast, complete lessons with Cassiel, do the gods knew what in Anevae's room afterward, go to dinner, and head back to her room for more fun and research. Things seemed to be going as well as they could. That was until one of the guards came to the training room one day during Anevae's lesson, stating her grandfather was requesting her appearance in the throne room. Reluctantly, I escorted her, and Maeyve followed.

I wonder what my grandfather wants now, said Anevae through our bond.

The only way we're going to find out is to show up, right? Maeyve said.

She's not wrong. There's no use in speculating when the answer already awaits us, I chimed in.

The rest of the walk was silent both in my mind and out...until Anevae's pulse began thudding in my ears. She was winding herself up too tight.

Stopping in the middle of the hall, I turned to face her just before she collided with me. I lightly grabbed her shoulders and said, "You need to calm down. All I can hear right now is your pulse going a million miles a minute. Take a deep breath for me."

She held my gaze and took a few deep breaths before rolling her shoulders back and nodding. Her heart rate had only slowed slightly. She was *not* ready yet. I raised my brow in a challenge.

I'm fine. The longer we stand here, the more we're prolonging things. Let's get on with it.

I love it when you're feisty, but you have to be careful with your grandfather. Take one more breath for me—like the good girl I know you can be—and then we can go. The sweet scent of her arousal filled my nostrils, and I groaned. *Baby, I don't think now is a good time for that. Take that breath, and let's go. Otherwise, I might have to punish you tonight.*

When she shifted from one foot to the other, I knew threatening her with punishment was *not* the right course of action. Her eyes bore into me, the blue intensifying.

Don't tempt me with a good time. I'd rather not deal with my grandfather right now anyway.

Maeyve crossed her arms, standing a few feet behind Anevae. *You realize I'm still here* and *can hear everything you're saying. I almost wish my mating with Emrhys hadn't merged our bonds. Hopefully, we can find a way to separate them when we want to. But right now, we need to go before someone sees you two standing here just looking into each other's eyes like the love-sick fools you are. Let's go.*

Why do you have to be right? Fuck. Fine. Let's go, I said, turning on the spot to continue down the hall.

Spoilsport, Anevae said.

Maeyve's irritation filtered through the bond as she said, *Are you guys serious right now? The last thing we need to happen is for someone to see something suspicious and report it to the king. Anevae is his granddaughter, and while she'd face punishment, it'd be nowhere near what we'd receive. He'd kill us in an instant, Emrhys.*

Rage simmered deep in my chest. Did she think none of us were aware of the consequences? Unfortunately, I didn't have a chance to ask her as we approached the throne room. When we reached the doors, the guards on duty bowed before opening them.

I stepped into the room, quickly moved to the side, and joined the bowing guards. As Anevae passed me, she bowed her head. A smirk appeared on my face, and her heart skipped a beat. I loved how my presence affected her.

"My sweet granddaughter! Thank you for joining us on such short notice." King Casimir said as he rose from his throne to greet her. When he reached the edge of the dias, he gestured toward the throne beside his, "Please have a seat. Eirian can sit on the other when she arrives."

After giving him a small curtsy, she did as he instructed. Once seated, Maeyve stood behind her throne on one side while I positioned myself on the other. Having her seated next to him on one of the thrones told me she wasn't in trouble but that he wanted to have her beside him while he took care of some business.

Just as we settled in our places, Eirian came barreling through the doors with Aeros hot on her heels. As she approached the dias, she paused, realizing where Anevae was seated. She clenched her jaw, and fury flashed in her silver eyes.

"That is my seat, Anevae. Move," Eirian growled.

Anevae shrugged. "Take that up with our dear grandfather. This is where he instructed me to sit."

Yellow took over Eirian's eyes, and their grandfather quickly rose to reprimand her. "That is enough! The throne Anevae is in is meant for the eldest. Eirian, please take your seat so that we may proceed."

Eirian lowered her head and curtsied as she mumbled, "Yes, Grandfather." Then, she strode to her seat, and Aeros flanked her as I'd done with Anevae.

The king took his seat again and straightened the lapels on his jacket. When he was done, he clapped his hands. "Bring them in."

A moment later, the doors flew open. Several guards surrounded two individuals. One was a woman with shoulder-length silver hair, while the other was a man with crimson red waves pushed back to keep out of his face. When the woman looked up, I stopped breathing for a moment.

Anevae and Eirian looked almost identical in terms of facial features, save for their eye and hair colors. Seeing the woman before us, I knew exactly where they got the majority of their features from. Her almond-shaped silver eyes were identical to Eirian's, and the color was the only difference for Anevae. The woman's nose was a smaller version of her daughters', and her lips were thinner, but I knew without a doubt this woman was their mother—Cordilaen.

The man was clearly their father—Roarc. His contribution to the girls was accentuating his wife's features, making their lips fuller and noses slightly bigger. Anevae had also gotten his red hair and blue eyes, although hers were a slightly different shade.

Once the group had entered the room, Anevae's parents were shoved to the ground. A growl rumbled from Roarc's chest. When he looked up toward the king, his blue irises glowed with a red rim around them.

"Now, now, Roarc. Be a good puppy," the king said in a teasing voice.

Cordilaen glared at the king. While she appeared calm, her eyes told another story. They weren't aglow with her magic, but rather, they glistened like she was on the brink of tears.

"Dear daughter, I'm so pleased to have you home—where you belong. Finally," the king said.

"I left this place long ago for a reason. I've only come to retrieve my daughters. They will be going home—to *their* home in the human realm. Don't make this about them when it's really about me," Cordilaen said, a hint of pain in her voice.

The king laughed. "This is where they belong. They are royalty, just as you are. All three of you belong here with me. We can all be a happy family again."

Cordilaen's jaw ticked. "Our family was never happy without my mother, and you know that. Throughout my childhood, you pawned me and Eve off on the nannies and servants every chance you could get. Then, when we got old enough, you took control of every aspect of our lives. I never left this castle, never socialized with anyone besides the servants and my teachers, all because you deemed it necessary. I will not let you do that to my girls. They deserve better than the solitude I was given."

The king waved a dismissive hand, "Don't be so dramatic. I gave you and your spoiled sister *everything* you could have ever wanted. And how did you both show your appreciation? You disobeyed my biggest rule: marry and mate one of our own. I expected it from your sister but not from you. Then, you went and made it nearly impossible to find you. You cannot take my granddaughters from me. They've never had access to their powers because you were giving them suppressants and keeping secrets from them! How do you expect them to leave *with you* when they are still furious *at you* for not telling them the truth? Being a parent isn't so easy, is it?"

"I kept them suppressed and away from this world because I didn't want you to find them. I wanted them to have a childhood unlike my own. But I should have known better. It was inevitable that you'd find them, or they'd stumble upon this world." A tear dropped from her eyes as she looked back at the floor. "Father, please. Let them go, and I will stay."

Roarc's gaze whipped to his wife. "Laeney, no."

Cordilaen shook her head. "Ro, I can't."

The king bellowed out a deep laugh. When he caught his breath, he said, "None of you will be leaving this realm again, Cordilaen. The damage has already been done, but your girls will compensate for your misdeeds. Now, the guards will escort you to your room so you can get cleaned up. Tonight, we shall celebrate your return."

Cordilaen scowled at the king. "What about Eve? I can't feel her, which means she's not here." When the king narrowed his eyes at her, she smiled. "You still don't know where she went, do you? You don't have your *whole* family back without her. And what if she had children? They would be your grandchildren, too."

The king's face flushed red. "I shunned her. She is not my daughter any longer. Not after she mated with that filthy demon, even after I forbade it. She knew what she was doing, and those who fraternize with her are not welcome here."

"Keep telling yourself that, father. I'm mated to Roarc, and yet here I am. You were looking for a reason to be free of her. No matter what, she is still your daughter."

The king shot to his feet and approached Cordilaen. She was still kneeling on the floor with her hands tied behind her back, but her chin was jutted out, and her jaw was clenched, screaming her defiance. When he reached her, he grabbed a handful of her hair and yanked her to her feet. "You will go to your room and get cleaned up for this celebration. Do not speak another word about your sister in my presence *ever again*. If you continue to disrespect me, you will not enjoy the punishment. Take your filthy puppy with you. I've invited his father to join us this evening."

After spitting out the last word, the king shoved his daughter toward one of the guards, who caught her and led her out of the room. When another guard reached for Roarc, he snapped at them. Doing the smart thing, they backed up, allowing Roarc to rise and follow his wife.

When we were excused, I rushed Anevae and Maeyve out, making it seem like I was taking them to their room. Instead, I pulled them into the training room and slammed the door behind us. The women looked confused, but I waved them off and searched for Cassiel.

What the fuck is going on? Maeyve asked.

We need to tell Cassiel that Anevae's parents are here, I said, still searching for the angel.

Maeyve crossed her arms as she watched me. Then, Anevae shoved past her and strode up to me. She touched my chest and whispered, "Stop for a moment, please."

When I did as she asked, she closed her eyes and took a deep breath, willing me to do the same. Instead, I stared at her. She was the calm in my storm.

We only stood there for a moment when Cassiel appeared next to her, looking frantic. "What's wrong? Are you okay? What happened?" he asked, reaching for her.

As she opened her eyes, tears streamed down her face. "They're here, Cass. My parents were brought in with their hands tied behind their backs like prisoners. He wants to have some sort of celebration this evening and invited my other grandfather as well. I'm scared."

Grabbing one of her hands from my chest, I brought it to my lips and gently kissed her knuckles. "The king won't harm them. Your mom means too much to him. And since your parents are mated, it's not likely the king would split them, but—"

"Let's deal with these things as they come. They just got here. Have you eaten your lunch yet?" Cassiel asked. Anevae shook her head, and he pulled her into his arms. "You need to eat. Let's get you to your room."

When we got there, Anevae went straight to the couch and began smoothing her skirt to give her hands something to do. Cassiel grabbed her plate and joined her, wanting to make sure she'd eat and to be there if she needed someone to comfort her.

Maeyve's shoulders slumped when Anevae leaned into Cassiel, and a deep ache echoed through our bond. She was used to being the one to comfort Anevae, but now that Anevae was mated to me and had opened up to Cassiel, she had to allow us to be there for her, too.

After a deep breath, Maeyve retrieved her lunch and curled up on the open couch. Wanting to remind her that she wasn't alone, I joined her, sitting beside her but putting my hand on her leg while she ate. She was mated to me, too, and I wouldn't run away or leave her like she was so worried about.

The women ate in silence, each with a mate to ground them. Once they seemed a little calmer, I moved to the window. Below me, servants hustled around, trying to prepare the gardens for the incoming guests.

Some of the fae below used their magic to enhance the foliage, while others rushed in and out of the ballroom to prepare for the king's festivities.

When Anevae was done eating, she put her plate on the table and sat back again. I took that as my cue to return to my seat so we could discuss our best course of action. The moment I sat, Maeyve put her plate next to Anevae's and leaned into me. I wrapped my arm around her to pull her close; it already felt so natural.

Anevae sighed as she looked at me, eyes glossy with unshed tears. I had to stop myself from rushing to her, to comfort her, and tell her everything would be okay. Just like Maeyve, I had to get comfortable sharing her. When she tried to speak, her lip trembled. A sob forced itself out as she leaned into Cassiel and let tears slide down her cheeks. That was the final straw. Maeyve and I approached, unable to sit back and watch her cry.

It's okay, baby. Give yourself a moment. Let your mind process the information at your pace, I said through our bond.

Take your time, my love, Maeyve said after me.

Cassiel sat there, comforting Anevae. Maeyve and I gave him the space to do that since he hadn't yet connected with her through a bond. I still wasn't sure what would happen when they did bond, though. He may only be bonded with her, or he may be able to join the group bond we'd formed without mating with Maeyve and me.

When Anevae stopped crying, she sat up and kissed Cassiel before pushing away from him. She turned her attention to Maeyve and me. Giving us a small smile, she caressed our cheeks. "Thank you all. I-I'm sorry. I don't know what is going to happen, and I really don't want to think about it. My parents are here now, meaning I'll have to face them, whether I like it or not. Fuck." She brushed away another tear as it fell.

"You're not facing this alone. All three of us are here. I won't leave your sight all evening, and I'm sure Maeyve won't either if she can help it," I said.

Cassiel added, "I'll attempt to stay nearby. We can't let everyone see all four of us together too often. Not to mention, I'm the outlier of the group. I have no reason to be near you outside of your lessons."

"I can't fucking stand this right now. I want to skip this *celebration*," she hissed, throwing her hands up in frustration.

I sighed and touched her hand when they were safely in her lap again. "I'm sorry to say you have to, or the king will have you dragged down there kicking and screaming. The man will get whatever he wants and do whatever he has to in order to get it. I don't think you want that kind of attention right now, do you?"

Anevae shook her head. "This is fucking ridiculous, and I'm going to complain the entire night. With that being said, Maeyve and I need a moment to get dressed. Once we're decent again, you guys can come back in."

With a sly grin, I said, "It's not like we haven't seen you both completely naked more than once. We've both touched your skin in the most delicate and delicious ways."

Both Anevae's and Maeyve's desires spiked as their heated gazes bore into me.

I was surprised when Maeyve was the one to say something and not Anevae. "If either of you is in here, we'll never make it to the celebration. Anevae and I like to kiss, and touch, and caress each other, but we can do all that *while* we get dressed and ready for this stupid thing. Can you say the same?"

My cock was hardening at the thought of them doing all those things. It made me want to stay in the room that much more, but Cassiel and I decided to comply with their request. After giving each of the girls a kiss, I hurried to my room to get ready...and maybe stroke one out so I wasn't so fucking hard the entire evening.

Chapter Thirty-Seven

Anevae

While Maeyve and I were in the shower, Maarya dropped off an intricate silver gown my grandfather had sent, requesting that I wear it to the ball. I had absolutely no intention of wearing it. Instead, Maeyve and I wore the simple, black ball gowns we'd asked Maarya for when she had clothes made for Maeyve weeks prior. I knew we'd be attending a ball at some point and wanted to be prepared when the time came.

I was nearly done getting ready when there was a knock on the door. Maeyve answered and inhaled sharply. Looking in the mirror before me, I caught sight of Emrhys. He was a sight for sore eyes dressed in all-black formal attire with red accents. His beard was nicely groomed, and his black hair was slicked back.

After taking turns admiring each other, our eyes met, and a smile crested his lips. *You look beautiful... Both of you do.*

You don't look too bad yourself, I said teasingly.

Loves, we need to be careful out there. If someone sees you guys looking at each other the way you are now, they'll know something is up between you two. Out there, Emrhys, you're Anevae's guard. I'm just her friend who's here to comfort her. We're not her lovers—or mates. Anevae is royalty, and the king will kill Emrhys and me if he finds out what we've done, Maeyve warned.

I rolled my eyes and got up from my chair at the vanity. *Don't remind me. I just want to stay in this room and keep you both to myself. If I see anyone looking at you the wrong way, I'm going to kill them, but I can't. And I need to act appropriately. Let's go.*

Emrhys tried to cover his smirk, but Maeyve and I shot him a look of warning.

He took a step back and threw his hands up in the air. *Sorry, sorry.*

That's what I thought. Now, be a good boy and take us to this stupid ball. Please? I said, batting my eyelashes at him.

The red in his eyes intensified as that damn smirk crept across his lips. *What happens if I'm a bad boy?*

I can't take either of you anywhere! Now, stop that, and let's go, Maeyve said as she stomped past us, throwing the door open.

Now you're the one not being any fun. What's wrong? You always joke around with me, I said, taking a tentative step toward her.

Maeyve stopped. *It's nothing to be concerned about right now. Can we just go, please? The faster we get this over with, the better.*

Talk to me, I pressed.

When she turned around, her eyes were glistening. *Don't worry about it right now.*

No, I said sternly.

Please, she pleaded.

My brows furrowed, and I crossed my arms. *Don't shut me out. There's something wrong, and I want to be able to help you, my love.*

I'm just incredibly nervous to go downstairs right now. There will be so many people who could possibly recognize me. I can't go back.

My heart sunk deep into my stomach. I hadn't forgotten about her time in the brothel but hadn't considered the high-profile targets she'd gone after who could attend the ball. *I'm so sorry. Just know that I will not let anything happen to you. Ever.*

Emrhys said, *Neither will I. Anyone who ever tries to harm you or take you from us will do so over my dead body. You are* our *mate. No one will ever touch you without your permission again.*

I looked at him and frowned. *Em—*

No. I will not let anything happen to either of you. We can blame it on being your guard or whatever the fuck you want, but first and foremost, you are both my *mates. Fuck everyone else. I will gladly die for either of you,* he said.

I wrapped my hands around his neck. "Please don't say that ever again. I can't imagine my life without you now. We'll figure this out, but please help me watch out for Maeyve right now."

Maeyve shifted uncomfortably behind me. I was worried about her. She'd never acted like this since I'd met her.

Emrhys put his hands on my hips and said, "I'll always watch out for our mate, princess. If we weren't expected downstairs soon, I'd suggest we go back into your room to calm her down. Unfortunately, your grandfather won't wait that long."

Before pulling away from me, he brushed his lips against mine in a soft, sweet kiss. I craved those intimate moments with my mates. But Maeyve was right; we needed to be more careful at the ball. I wondered if I could keep her hidden if I had control of my glamour magic. I shook the thought from my mind. I needed to make my appearance at this stupid ball.

Maeyve and I followed Emrhys to the stairs. Emrhys stepped to the side when we reached the top, and trumpets announced my presence to the crowd below. Everyone's attention shifted to me, and my eyes grew wide. There were so many people before me.

With my eyes lost to the crowd, I didn't see the man beside Emrhys, and when he introduced me, I jumped. "Presenting Her Highness, Anevae Rilvara, eldest daughter of Princess Cordilaen and granddaughter of King Casimir and Queen Ahmeira, may she rest in peace."

Everyone in the crowd below dipped into bows and curtsies. But when they rose, hushed conversations began. They likely had a lot of questions, seeing as this was my first introduction to the public. I wasn't sure what to think.

When Emrhys began his descent down the stairs, I grabbed Maeyve's hand to make sure she stayed close. As we weaved through the crowd, they gave us a wide berth but made no move to cover their stares. Many of those around me didn't know I existed before my introduction. I ignored them; they didn't know me, and I didn't care what they thought.

Maeyve tried to pull her hand from mine numerous times as we walked, but I wouldn't let go. I knew something was wrong when her panic-filled voice was in my mind. *Anevae, please let my hand go. Everyone is staring at us. I can't afford to draw attention to myself in this crowd. I'm sorry, my love. I want to hold your hand so badly, but I can't go back to that brothel...I can't leave you.*

My heart sank again. It hurt to know how worried she was about Madam Tanith and returning to that awful place. Then, irritation spiked. In Caellaias, I had power. I was the daughter of a princess. So, while I didn't have the royal title, I did have a say in things. *As long as I live, I will never let you go back there. You are mine, and your rightful place is beside me. I don't give a fuck what anyone says. If someone tries to interfere with that, they will meet my wrath.*

Princess, I know you're irritated, but you need to calm down. Your magic is stirring, Emrhys said.

I don't give a fuck! Let it stir. Let people see how powerful I am. Let them fear me.

Love, you don't want them to fear you, Maeyve said.

Says who? I don't care if they fear me. Fuck them all.

Emrhys' voice was stern with his response. *You should care. You're stuck here for the foreseeable future. One thing you should know about this kingdom is its inhabitants look up to the rulers. Whether you like it or not, you're royalty,; soon they'll start looking up to you, too.*

Ugh. I already fucking hate this place. Maeyve, nothing will happen to you. If anything seems suspicious, just tell us. Let's get this night over with.

Emrhys led us to an elegant ballroom, where my arrival was announced yet again. My jaw dropped as I took in the room before me. Several elaborate crystal chandeliers hung from the ceiling, illuminating the room with bright lights. Dozens of tables were arranged around the dance floor where various beings floated across it doing dances I'd never seen before. Across the room, my grandfather sat on the raised dais behind a long table in a smaller version of his throne, with orletaylear-tipped spires jutting above his head. To his right was my mom and two other ornate seats for Eiri and me. To his left was a smaller version of the queen's throne—where my grandmother would've sat if she was still alive.

My father's absence caught me off-guard at first. But in the eyes of my grandfather, he was not an acceptable mate for my mother and, therefore, was likely not invited to sit at the table. In front of his subjects, the king would do everything in his power to keep my parents separated. He didn't want to be embarrassed by his precious daughter and her inability to obey his commands.

I found my dad at a table near the steps of the dais, staring down at his hands. They were laced together on the table, cleaner than I'd ever seen them before. I never knew what he did for work, but I knew he wasn't a white-collar worker by any means—the hours he worked and constantly being called in at the drop of a hat made that clear to me. His hair was slicked back the way it always was, but when he looked up, his black eye caught my attention first. If he'd had it in the throne room, I hadn't noticed it. Before he looked away, my eyes drifted to his neck, catching a glimpse of the black collar.

What the hell? I thought to myself.

He must've really pissed off your grandfather to get that, Emrhys said nonchalantly.

Furrowing my brows, I stared daggers into his back. *What is it exactly?*

It's a collar that different types of magic can influence. He's being forced into submission by your grandfather who is allowing your mother's personal guards to treat him as they please. Your grandfather is trying to get to your mom, too. He wants to break her—to make sure she knows who's actually in charge here, Emrhys explained.

I clenched and unclenched my jaw, trying to keep my magic locked down when I reached the dais. Meeting my grandfather's gaze, I curtsied deeply. Keeping my cool would be a lot harder than I anticipated when his eyes darkened.

"You look beautiful, dear granddaughter, but I believe I sent a different gown to your room for the evening," he said, venom dripping from his tone that only those close would recognize.

Bowing my head, I said, "Alas, Grandfather, I spilled some wine on it while trying it on. I knew it wouldn't look good for me to come down in a dress that was dirtied. My apologies."

My grandfather clenched his jaw and let out a breath before speaking. "I see. If that were to happen again, please call for Maarya to fetch another or get the fabric cleaned at once."

"Understood, Grandfather. I did not want to bother her. I was certain she was busy preparing for this gathering."

"Indeed she was, but she can always be called upon for whatever you need. That is her job. Please join your mother and me on the dais. Your mu—" He stopped himself and cleared his throat before motioning to the table my father occupied, "Maeyve may have a seat with your...father. Emrhys, please take your position on the stairs."

Maeyve and I nodded as I curtsied, and she bowed.

Before I could walk away, her voice was in my head. *I'm a thought away, my love.*

I bit my lip piercing to hide the smile that desperately wanted to crest my lips. *Please behave and try not to terrorize my father too much.*

Aww. Where's the fun in that? she asked. I knew if I looked at her, she'd give me big puppy dog eyes, which only made me want to laugh more.

Maeyve, behave or no fun later. Also, stop making me want to laugh; people will think I'm crazy if I start randomly laughing at myself.

I'll just drive Emrhys crazy instead.

You realize she's still going to hear you, right? Emrhys asked.

Fine. I'll just sit there like the perfect angel I am and not talk at all.

Maeyve, Emrhys growled, and even in my mind, the tone had me soaking wet.

Finally listening to our mate, she hurried to join my dad. Even though she was trying to lighten the mood, I was so wound up and worried about the situation we'd found ourselves in. We still had so much to work out. I tried to force it from my mind as I reached my seat. Azur was there to ensure I got settled but then promptly left.

I refused to acknowledge my mom, even though she was beside me. Instead, I got lost in the intricacies of the dancers before me. Their feet seemed to barely touch the floor as they glided across the polished wood.

"I'm sorry, my Lily. I should have told you both about this world directly. This is all my fault," my mom whispered.

Ice trickled through my veins. "You're sorry? At least you told us about Caellaias. The one I want an apology from is him," I said as I nodded at my dad.

"He thought he was doing what was best for you."

"And the best way you *both* thought to keep us safe was to keep our powers from us? To not prepare us for this world?" I began but then stopped myself and took a deep breath. "You know what? This isn't a discussion I want to have right now. We're going to be stuck in Caellaias for a while, so we can discuss this at another time...when both of your children are here for it *and* can actively participate. As of right now, I have nothing else to say to you."

"I understand. Who is that woman sitting with your father? She arrived with you, correct?"

Looking at the table, I bit my lip. How much could I tell my mom without giving away too much information? How much could I tell her without my grandfather finding something out? "You remember that house Eiri saw on the way to mine?" My mom nodded, and I continued, "She was living there."

"Why is she here with you? She isn't human, is she?"

I shook my head as I met Maeyve's gaze. "She's not human. She actually helped me get here...to rescue Eiri, but things changed significantly with that."

My mom shifted her gaze to Maeyve and gasped. I whipped my head in her direction, the question I wanted to ask written all over my face. "I apologize. I was just startled. Her eyes are...interesting. If she is not human, what is she?"

I furrowed my brow and went on the defense. "She's half fox shifter and half succubus."

"That is a...strange mix."

"It is, but she's a wonderful woman. Anyway, I wonder where Eiri is. I would have thought she'd been here by now."

As if the mere thought of her could bring her into existence, my sister approached the dais, led by Aeros, in a gown matching the one my grandfather had sent to my room. After deeply curtsying, she said, "Hello, Grandfather. Thank you for the dress; it's lovely."

The king gave her a wide smile. "I am glad you like it. It is too bad your sister could not wear hers. However, I digress. Please take your seat next to her. And Aeros, please join Emrhys in guarding the stairs. Now that we are all here, the festivities can begin."

After another deep curtsy, she made her way up the dais to take her seat beside me, acting as if I wasn't there. I didn't mind; I was fed up with her attitude toward me when all I'd done was try to rescue her from our evil grandfather. His niceties had blinded her, and it disgusted me.

Clearing my mind, I shifted my focus back to the ball itself. Dealing with my sister was a battle for another day.

Chapter Thirty-Eight

Anevae

After Eiri arrived, things settled down for a little while. Several different kinds of beings approached the dais to show off their talents, but I wasn't interested. Having been sandwiched between my mom and my sister made me uncomfortable. I was boxed in by the two people I trusted with almost anything, only to find out they'd lied to me—betrayed me.

To distract myself from examining the life I thought I knew, I glanced at the table with Maeyve and my dad. Maeyve was on guard, likely watching for anyone who might recognize her, while my dad stared down at his hands, shoulders still slumped. I'd never thought anyone could break him, but the king seemed to know his weaknesses and exploited them to the fullest extent.

Have you talked to him at all? I asked Maeyve. She shook her head only enough that someone really looking at her could see. *Have you tried to talk to him?* I asked, and again, she shook her head. Sighing, I said, *I'm sorry, my love. For putting you in this position.*

There's no need for you to apologize. You didn't ask for this.

I know, but you're on constant high alert because we're stuck here—because you came with me when I told you that you didn't have to.

Anevae, stop. There's nothing we can do about the past, but we can focus on the future. Let's just do that, okay?

Gritting my teeth, I said, *Fine. I hope this fucking ball is over soon.*

Emrhys' voice cut in, *I hate to remind you that you haven't even been fed yet, sweetheart.*

Fucking seriously? When will the food be served? Is this going to be like every dinner I've gone to for the last few weeks with multiple damn courses?

Yes, Princess. That's how all the dinners and balls work here. It'll be okay.

Is my other grandfather here? Amaroc?

He's not yet, but I will keep an eye out for him and let you know when he arrives.

Thank you, Em.

Of course, Princess. That's what I'm here for.

That's not the only reason you're here, and you know it. I freaking wish we could go back to my room right now. I'm so uncomfortable sitting here in front of all these people. I've never been one to enjoy being the center of attention, I whined.

Soon, we'll get to go, love, Maeyve said.

I sat there, fidgeting with my hands for several more minutes before the dancers cleared the floor and dinner was served. As always, it tasted delicious, but I honestly missed the food from the human realm more than I could explain. I missed the human realm as a whole and the ability to do what I wanted without fighting someone or another.

When dinner was finished, my grandfather stood and called attention to himself while the kitchen staff rounded up the empty plates. "Thank you all for joining me this evening to celebrate the return of my family. My sweet Cordilaen has returned with her daughters, Anevae and Eirian. Their presence in Caellaias fills my heart with nothing but joy. I cannot explain how much I have missed my daughter over the years. With my granddaughters here, my world is now complete." Leaning down, he picked up his champagne flute and held it up. "Let us toast to the joy family brings to our lives."

Everyone dutifully raised their glasses, not having any semblance of an idea that the family he loved so much was being held against their will. If they'd known, would they have raised their glasses then? They were so devoted to their king, I was sure they would've.

After my grandfather's toast, the festivities of the evening continued. My mom made no move to speak to me after I'd shut her down, and Eiri seemed content to ignore me. I was getting antsy; I'd never done well sitting in one place for too long.

Leaning forward, I asked, "May I go dance, Grandfather?"

"If you wish to. Emrhys, please escort Anevae to the dance floor. She may need a little assistance. I'm not sure she's ever been taught our dances."

Emrhys appeared at my side and bowed. "Yes, Your Majesty." Then, he held out his hand. "Come with me, please, Your Highness."

When I stood, I took his hand and let him lead me to the dance floor. I was grateful my grandfather had asked Emrhys to dance with me. If it'd been anyone else, I would've backed out; I didn't trust anyone, and I wasn't sure Maeyve knew the dances either.

Once we reached the dance floor, Emrhys pulled me into him. I tried to put space between us, but he pulled me closer.

Em, my grandfather can see us, I warned him.

We're just dancing. Nothing else. I need you close to make sure you don't fall. Plus, Maeyve can warn us if he starts getting suspicious.

Okay, well, be warned that I have two left feet.

Glancing down at me, he cocked his head ever so slightly. *You...have two left feet? I'm pretty sure you have a right and a left the last time I looked.*

I let out a breathy laugh. *It's an expression. It means I'm really clumsy and trip over my own feet all too often.*

That's a strange expression. Anyway, just follow my lead.

Careful not to step on his feet, we glided across the dance floor like I'd seen the dancers doing before. It was a magical feeling, and I didn't want it to stop.

We continued for several minutes before I glanced at the table where most of my family sat. As Emrhys twirled me, I caught a glimpse of blonde hair. I hadn't seen any servants around with blonde hair recently, but that didn't mean it couldn't have been a guard making his rounds or something.

Em, can we get closer to the dais for a moment, please? There's a man up there I want to look at a little closer. He seems…familiar somehow.

Emrhys did as I asked, slowly getting us closer to the dais without making it seem suspicious. As we got closer, the man's features became clearer. He wore emerald green formal attire that went well with his wavy blonde hair. He didn't appear stocky or buff like most of the guards in the castle, but he wasn't thin and lanky like many of the commoners. Who was he? And how was he speaking with my grandfather so closely?

After another twirl, I got a good look at the man, and my heart stopped for a split second. With complete attention on the dais, I tripped over Emrhys' foot. We came to a grinding halt as Emrhys caught me and put me back on my feet.

All the air had left my body.

I couldn't move—couldn't breathe.

Placing his hands on my shoulders, Emrhys asked, "Are you okay?"

I-I have to get out of here. Get me out of here, please?

What's wrong? Emrhys asked.

The man speaking with my grandfather…he shouldn't be here. My father told me he took care of him years ago.

I couldn't answer Emrhys. He didn't know as much about my past as Maeyve did; I never thought he'd need to know about this.

But then the man on the dais looked in my direction, and ice flooded my veins.

It's Ambrose.

About the author

Mikaelynn Rose is a hard-working, devoted woman whose world revolves around an amazing little boy...well, I guess her husband, too. While she lives just outside of Denver with her high school sweetheart and son, she'd much rather be in the country or the mountains. When she's not working, she's writing, reading, listening to music, spending time with her loved ones, and, of course, drinking way too much coffee for her own good.

Find me on my socials!

f facebook.com/mikaelynnrose/

♪ tiktok.com/@mikaelynnrose

♪ tiktok.com/@author.mikaelynn.rose

⃝ instagram.com/mikaelynnrose

g goodreads.com/mikaelynnrose

www.ingramcontent.com/pod-product-compliance
Lightning Source LLC
Chambersburg PA
CBHW020033310726
48970CB00007B/2245